W9-BNT-960

"I just don't want you to think you can make excuses for reneging on a deal."

China stopped with a forkful of omelet halfway to her mouth. "What deal? We haven't made a deal."

Campbell appeared unconcerned by her denial. "It wasn't written and signed, but there damn well is a deal going on here, and you know it. Had we been alone when you woke up this morning, we'd be in bed now and not giving a damn about breakfast."

He spoke with complete honesty, and while she admired that, she couldn't quite match it. She put the bite of omelet in her mouth to buy time.

"It would have been a mistake," she said finally.

Campbell leaned even closer to China. "When you get your courage back," he said, his voice very quiet, "I'll show you that making love with me would never be a mistake."

Dear Reader,

Campbell Abbott is a man trying to find his own identity. His eldest brother, Killian, is a brilliant businessman, and Sawyer, his second brother, is a courageous daredevil. Campbell is the product of their father's second marriage, and has always felt inferior because his dreams are smaller than those of his brothers.

China Grant has just discovered that she isn't who she thought she was. Though she loves the Abbotts and they want to take her in as part of their family, she has a desperate need to unearth her real past before she can plan her future.

Campbell and China are making a common mistake. They think that love, like most other things in life, requires a solid foundation on which to build. I've tried to prove with this book that that isn't true. Love can come to life on the smallest invitation, grow in conditions that would support nothing else we know of, and flourish when everything else is dying. It can live when the bottom's fallen out of the world and there's nothing to hold on to. It depends upon nothing for its survival but the willingness that it be there—or maybe the determination.

I hope you enjoy Campbell and China's adventures on the road to that discovery.

My best wishes!

Muriel Jensen

P.O. Box 1168
Astoria, Oregon 97103

HIS FAMILY
Muriel Jensen

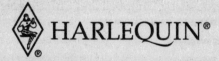

HARLEQUIN®

TORONTO • NEW YORK • LONDON
AMSTERDAM • PARIS • SYDNEY • HAMBURG
STOCKHOLM • ATHENS • TOKYO • MILAN • MADRID
PRAGUE • WARSAW • BUDAPEST • AUCKLAND

If you purchased this book without a cover you should be aware
that this book is stolen property. It was reported as "unsold and
destroyed" to the publisher, and neither the author nor the
publisher has received any payment for this "stripped book."

ISBN 0-373-75070-6

HIS FAMILY

Copyright © 2005 by Muriel Jensen.

All rights reserved. Except for use in any review, the reproduction or
utilization of this work in whole or in part in any form by any electronic,
mechanical or other means, now known or hereafter invented, including
xerography, photocopying and recording, or in any information storage
or retrieval system, is forbidden without the written permission of the
publisher, Harlequin Enterprises Limited, 225 Duncan Mill Road,
Don Mills, Ontario M3B 3K9, Canada.

All characters in this book have no existence outside the imagination of
the author and have no relation whatsoever to anyone bearing the same
name or names. They are not even distantly inspired by any individual
known or unknown to the author, and all incidents are pure invention.

This edition published by arrangement with Harlequin Books S.A.

® and TM are trademarks of the publisher. Trademarks indicated with
® are registered in the United States Patent and Trademark Office, the
Canadian Trade Marks Office and in other countries.

www.eHarlequin.com

Printed in U.S.A.

Books by Muriel Jensen

HARLEQUIN AMERICAN ROMANCE

* Millionaire, Montana
** The Abbotts

Don't miss any of our special offers. Write to us at the following address for information on our newest releases.

Harlequin Reader Service
U.S.: 3010 Walden Ave., P.O. Box 1325, Buffalo, NY 14269
Canadian: P.O. Box 609, Fort Erie, Ont. L2A 5X3

THE ABBOTTS—A GENEALOGY

Thomas and Abigail Abbott: arrived on the *Mayflower*; raised sheep outside Plymouth

William and Deborah Abbott: built a woolen mill in the early nineteenth century

Jacob and Beatrice Abbott: ran the mill and fell behind the competition when they failed to modernize

James and Eliza Abbott: Jacob's eldest son and grandfather of Killian, Sawyer and Campbell Abbott; married a cotton heiress from Virginia

Nathan Abbott and Susannah Stewart Abbott: parents of Killian and Sawyer; Nathan diversified to boost the business and married Susannah, the daughter of a Texas oilman who owned Bluebonnet Knoll

Nathan Abbott and Chloe Marceau: parents of Campbell and Abigail; renamed Bluebonnet Knoll and made it Shepherd's Knoll

Killian Abbott: now the CEO of Abbott Mills; married to **Cordelia Magnolia Hyatt**

Sawyer Abbott: Killian's brother by blood; a daredevil

Campbell Abbott: half brother to Killian and Sawyer; manages the Abbott estate on Long Island

China Grant: thinks she might be the missing Abigail

Sophie Foster: mother of Gracie, Eddie and Emma Foster; the woman with whom Sawyer Abbott falls in love

Brian Girard: half brother to Killian and Sawyer

Chapter One

Campbell Abbott put an arm around China Grant's shoulders and walked her away from the fairground picnic table and into the trees. She was sobbing and he didn't know what to do. He wasn't good with women. Well, he was, but not when they were crying.

"I was so *sure!*" she said in a fractured voice.

He squeezed her shoulders. "I know. I'm sorry."

She sobbed, sniffed, then speculated, "I don't suppose DNA tests are ever wrong?"

"I'm certain that's possible," he replied, "but I'm also certain they were particularly careful with this case. Everyone on Long Island is aware that the Abbotts' little girl was kidnapped as a toddler. The possibility that you might be her, returned after twenty-five years, had everyone hoping the test would be positive."

"Except you." It surprised him that she spoke without rancor. In the month since she'd turned up at Shepherd's Knoll looking for her family, he'd done his best to make things difficult for her. In the beginning he'd simply doubted her claims, certain any enterprising young woman could buy a toddler's blue corduroy rompers at a used-clothing store and claim she was an Abbott Mills heiress because she had an outfit similar to what the child was wearing when she'd been taken. As he'd told his older brothers repeatedly, Abbott Mills had made thousands, possibly millions, of those corduroy rompers.

Campbell had wanted her to submit to a DNA test then and there. If she was Abigail, he was her full sibling and therefore would be a match.

But Chloe, his mother, had been in Paris at the time, caring for a sick aunt, and Killian, his oldest half brother, hadn't wanted to upset her further. He'd suggested they wait until Chloe returned home.

Sawyer, his other half brother, had agreed. Accustomed to being outvoted by them most of his life, Campbell had accepted his fate when Killian further suggested that China stay on to help Campbell manage the Abbott estate until Chloe came home. Killian was CEO of Abbott Mills, and Sawyer headed the Abbott Mills Foundation.

Killian and Sawyer were the products of their father's first marriage to a Texas oil heiress. Campbell and the missing Abigail were born to his second wife, Chloe, a former designer for Abbott Mills.

When Chloe had come back from Paris two weeks ago, the test had been taken immediately. While everyone had been preparing for the hospital fund-raiser that had just taken place that afternoon and evening, China had been at the house alone when the results had arrived by courier. So she'd brought the sealed envelope with her and opened it just moments ago, when the family had been all together at the picnic table after the fund-raiser.

They'd all expected a very different result. That China couldn't be related to the Abbotts had been an unhappy surprise. His mother was heartbroken, his siblings saddened, the other women in their family upset. Even Campbell felt…well, ambivalent about it.

The late-July evening was warm and redolent of fairground food and salt water. He could even smell the ripening apples at Shepherd's Knoll. For reasons he couldn't explain, his senses were sharpened tonight.

China took several steps away from him and he was able to study her without the suspicion and confusion that usually permeated his thoughts when it had seemed she was his sister. He noted the trim body in the short denim skirt and yellow T-shirt, the cloud of dark hair.

She turned to him, her dark eyes shiny with tears, the soft line of her mouth uncertain. "I'm sure this validates all your suspicions that I'm just a moneygrubbing opportunist."

He'd once believed that. He couldn't imagine that Abby would turn up after all this time and relieve the anguish that was at the heart of all their lives.

He'd been only five when she was taken, but he bore as much pain and guilt as everyone in the family did. He remembered clearly that his fourteen-month-old sister had toddled into his room that afternoon, fascinated by the fleet of large yellow trucks that were his pride and joy. He'd occasionally let her play with them, but that particular day he'd been banned from a football game Killian and Sawyer were playing in the backyard with their friends. They'd said he was too small and might be hurt.

Feelings injured, he'd passed on his annoyance to Abby, wresting one of his trucks from her and inadvertently bruising her arm when he yanked it away. His mother had come and carried her out of his room. His last memory of her was of her weeping face over his mother's shoulder. The image of it had haunted him for years.

He wondered now if that had been partially responsible for his animosity toward China—a sort of transference of guilt.

"No, of course it doesn't," he said. "I'd come to the point where I was convinced you knew what you were talking about. The evidence was there."

Her face crumpled and she turned away, leaning a shoulder against the slender gray trunk of a birch tree. "Instead, it appears you were right. Abbott Mills must have made a million of those rompers."

Curiously, even after the convincing proof of a scientific test, he still felt connected to her. He walked around the tree and offered her his handkerchief. "There's still the matter of the newspaper clippings. Why would those have been saved, if they weren't somehow related to you?"

China had been adopted by a California couple through their doctor, who'd also found them a second child. The girls had been raised together, and when their widowed father died just a few months before, they'd been cleaning out the house for sale and found boxes with their names on them in the attic.

"I don't understand," she said, dabbing at her eyes, then

her nose. She sniffed and tossed her head back. "I thought I had the truth, but I was wrong. I should go home."

"You realize you're welcome to stay as long as you like."

"Thank you, but now that we all know I'm not Abigail, there's little point in my being here. It was all right when we weren't sure, but now that we are…"

"Who's going to look after the estate?" he asked, sure his mother would be upset if she left. The entire family had grown attached to China. "I'm supposed to report to work at Flamingo Gables in a week. The family's getting used to counting on you."

He saw her draw a breath and straighten away from the tree. She was firming her resolve. "I have my own business in California. My own…my own…life, such as it is."

She looked suddenly bereft, and he was surprised to find that he couldn't stand it. He had a way to shake her out of it. "Shopping," he said. "It's not as though you provide food or shelter for the needy. You go shopping for the rich. They can do without you for a while."

She bristled with indignation. "I've told you repeatedly that I work for the busy, not the rich, and aiding them to save money on things they require may even help them give to food banks and shelters for the needy!"

"Sure. My point is, you shouldn't make a decision without thinking it through."

"I'm going home," she said firmly, and started back through the trees the way they'd come.

He'd been wondering how to bring up a detail to all this that apparently hadn't occurred to her. As she hurried away from him, he felt certain it was time to just say it. "What about your sister?" he asked, following her.

"What about her?"

"Have you ever considered that she could be connected to us?"

"What?" She stopped in her tracks, holding back the tensile branch of a vine maple to frown at him. "What are you talking about?"

"Haven't you thought that…maybe…your box is really hers?"

She appeared shocked by that suggestion, then her eyes lost focus as she thought it over.

"You said your boxes were the same," he prodded.

"Yes," she said.

"Exactly the same?"

"Exactly." She still didn't seem to see his point. "But my name was on mine, and her name…"

"Yes, but what if somewhere along the line, the lids got switched?" Her eyes widened as she considered that possibility. "And what's in her box is really yours, and what's in the box with your name on it is really hers?"

Her brow furrowed as she came to see that as a possibility.

"It could have happened any number of ways," he went on, subtly reeling her in. "Did you ever move when you were growing up?"

"Twice," she replied. "Friends of my father's helped us."

"Could have happened then. The boxes fell over, and the lids got mixed up. Or maybe one of your parents adding something to the boxes inadvertently did it."

She stared into his eyes with a sort of horrified awe. "That's…grasping at straws."

"Is it?" He held the branch for her when her fingers grew lax and a branch was about to scratch her face. "You were convinced by the old clippings that they must have been intended for you. But since the test proved that wrong, then the other possibility doesn't seem that far off, does it?" He let that sink in for a minute. "If the clippings weren't for you, then who else is there?"

CHINA WOULD HAVE liked to push him onto the fragrant grass. Since the day she'd first set eyes on him, he'd stood determinedly in her way. He didn't believe she was his little sister returned; didn't believe she wanted no money, just family; blocked at every turn her attempts to be friends with him. Even now, when all she wanted to do was leave, he put up another roadblock.

She didn't want to stay another minute, was embarrassed and disappointed that she'd turned everyone's life upside down quite needlessly, as it turned out. But what if he was right? What if, somehow, the lids of the boxes had gotten mixed up and her adopted sister, Janet, was their flesh-and-blood sister?

She met Campbell Abbott's dark gaze. He stood there like the locked gate he'd been since she'd arrived—an inch or two shorter than his brothers, but broader in the shoulders, and more inclined to seriousness than they were. He'd prevented her from ever feeling completely welcome, and now he wanted to prevent her from leaving!

She turned away, headed for the parking lot. "I'll

call her and tell her to get in touch with you," she shouted back at him.

He caught her arm at the edge of the parking lot and turned her to him. "You can't do that," he said with surprising gentleness. "You can't just take off on Mom. We all have to talk this out. Come to a solution. And if your sister is our sister, you can't expect to be able to stay out of it."

She *could* expect to, but of course it wouldn't happen.

Janet was prettier, smarter, loved by everyone for her unfailing good humor and quick wit. China had never resented her for it, only envied her. China was basically shy, but inclined to speak her mind if the situation warranted. The courage she'd required to present herself to the Abbotts as possibly their daughter/sister returned had been huge.

Her grief that she wasn't theirs was softened somewhat now by the suggestion that Janet might be Abigail. China and Janet had squabbled as children but come to appreciate each other as they grew older. Though Janet had the brains and the boys, China had the domestic skills that kept their home going after their mother died.

They now loved and respected each other, and the last time they'd been together, before each had set off to solve the mystery of her cardboard box, they'd vowed that whatever came of their searches, they would be sisters forever.

"China." Campbell spoke quietly as his family hurried toward them en masse. "You can't leave them yet. Please."

There was something to be said for having reality

thrust upon you. It seemed to alter time. Just fifteen minutes ago, she'd been sure she was Abigail Abbott and
the report she was about to open would prove it.

Now it seemed as though that moment had been
aeons ago. She was not an Abbott. She was still China
Grant, the same woman she'd always been. The heady
excitement of discovery had been doused, but there was
something comforting about familiarity.

Chloe threw her arms around her and held her closely. "You must not leave," she said, her voice tight with
emotion. "We're all agreed. You may not be my daughter, but you've become an important part of the family."

Chloe leaned back to look into China's eyes, her own
sweet and pleading. China opened her mouth to reply, but
Chloe interrupted. "Yes, I know you have a life of your
own. A small business you must keep track of. But we
need you, too. Killian tells me you've done a wonderful
job helping run the estate, and if Campbell chooses to
leave us to conquer new horizons, then you must stay and
help us until we find someone to replace him, *oui?*"

China would have loved nothing more than to make
a little niche for herself with the warm and wild Abbotts,
but it didn't seem fair to the real Abigail. Especially if
that was Janet. But maybe she did have to stay long
enough to help them determine if indeed she was.

"I'll stay until I can find my sister, Janet, for you,"
she said.

When that met with a confused expression from the
rest of the family now pressed around them, Campbell
explained his theory about the boxes.

Killian and Sawyer, both with the fair good looks of

their father's first wife, frowned at each other, then at Campbell. "You really think this possible?" Killian asked.

Campbell made a noncommittal gesture. "Seems that way to me. How else would you explain that China has everything in that box that would relate her to us, but she isn't Abby? Yet she has a sister the same age, adopted at about the same time, who's gone off on her own quest with a box identical except for the contents?"

Sawyer raised an eyebrow. "He might have a point," he said to Killian. "You don't think he's smarter than us, after all, do you?"

"Never happened," Killian grinned. "Well, how do we find your sister, China?"

China tried to remember the town in Canada's north mentioned on the birth certificate in Janet's box. That was where Janet had intended to begin her search. "Somewhere in the Northwest Territories. I can't remember the town, but she's staying at an inn there— I have the name and number written down in my book at the house. I'll call tonight."

China was suddenly flanked by Cordie, Killian's pregnant wife, and Sophie, who was engaged to marry Sawyer. They led her toward the Abbotts' limousine, with Sophie's daughters—Gracie, 10, and Emma, 5— dancing along ahead of them. Sophie's seven-year-old son, Eddie, hung back with the men. "You have to stay for the wedding," Sophie said. "We're thinking about Labor Day."

"Oh, I…" China tried to formulate an excuse, certain she could locate Janet, stay just long enough for the DNA test, then find a graceful way to leave.

"I need you for a bridesmaid." Sophie, who'd grabbed China's hand, tightened her grip.

"And you won't want to leave without seeing my babies." That was Cordie. Her babies weren't due for another four months.

China let them talk, smiling cooperatively at all their suggestions of what she must do, privately making plans to be gone within two and a half weeks at the most. Three days to get Janet here from wherever she was and tested, then two weeks for the results of the test.

Daniel, the Abbotts' chauffeur, opened the door of the long black Lincoln and the women piled inside, along with Daniel's wife Kezia, the Abbotts' cook and house-keeper. Killian lifted Tante Bijou out of her wheelchair and into the other side, while Sawyer folded the chair and put it in the trunk.

Chloe, tucked into the facing seat with China, wrapped an arm around her and patted her shoulder. "All will be well," she promised with the determined smile China had grown used to since Chloe had been home. "Trust me on this."

"I'll call Janet right away," China promised.

"I mean," Chloe corrected, "that all will be well with you."

China smiled and nodded politely, knowing Chloe wanted her to feel a part of their family. While she appreciated that, she'd just received irrefutable proof that she wasn't. It would be hard to explain to anyone how bereft she felt.

It wasn't as though she'd had an unhappy childhood. The Grants had been loving and kind to her and Janet.

She didn't remember specifically being told she was adopted; it was as though she'd always known. Her father had told her over and over that she and her sister were special because they'd been "chosen."

Still, she'd felt the need to know where she'd come from. Her mother had always said that she knew nothing about their natural families, only that the doctor through which they'd adopted the girls said China's mother had been a single woman dying of cancer, and Janet's mother, also single, had been killed in an automobile accident.

They'd always accepted that, and neither had ever instituted a search for their biological parents for fear of upsetting their adoptive parents. Then they'd discovered the boxes in the attic and realized that what they'd been told wasn't true.

It suddenly occurred to China that if Campbell's theory was correct, the truth about her life was somewhere in Janet's box. Somewhere in northern Canada.

IN HER BEDROOM overlooking the back lawn, part of the apple orchard and the small house where Daniel and Kezia lived, China sat at the antique desk, trying to decipher her sister's handwriting. She'd received a forwarded letter from Janet just a week ago. It was brief and to the point.

I'm staying at the Little Creek House Hotel near Fort Providence. I've finally tracked the godmother's name on the birth certificate to this town. Very thinly populated. Have learned she went to live with her son, but no one I've talked to so far knows where that is. Got my work cut out for me, I guess. Hope you're having better luck. Love, Jan.

She'd included the telephone number of the hotel.

A cheerful masculine voice answered. "Little Creek."

"Hello. May I speak to Janet Grant, please?" China asked.

"I'm afraid she's away for several days," the man replied. "May I take a message?"

"Away?" China repeated.

"Yes. She's hired a guide and gone to Jasper's Camp. It's several days by foot. I'm afraid there's no cell phone reception there." He again offered to take a message.

"Ah…yes. Would you ask her to phone her sister, please?" She gave him her cell-phone number, as well as the number there at Shepherd's Knoll on the chance Janet had misplaced them.

"Yes, of course. As soon as she returns. Guaranteed to be a few days, at least."

"Thank you."

China groaned as she hung up the phone. She had a terrible feeling this was not going to happen quickly. She couldn't imagine where Jasper's Camp was, but if Janet had had to hire a guide to go there…

She tried to imagine her beautiful stockbroker sister going anywhere that required three days on foot, and grew worried. She also felt great pangs of guilt. Janet had no idea she was probably tracking down China's roots, and that her own might very well be right here in Losthampton.

China prepared to go downstairs where she could hear the Abbotts talking over wine and popcorn, and tell them that she really wasn't sure where Janet was but that she'd left a message.

More waiting. She hoped they would take it better than she was able to, as she wondered who her family were.

Chapter Two

"I do not see how you can make plans to leave forever when we may have found your sister after twenty-five years and I've been home just two weeks." Chloe Abbott marched across her bedroom, the dark blue lace coat of a peignoir set billowing after her. She gave Campbell an injured, accusing look over her shoulder. "It's thoughtless, inconsiderate and…and neither of your brothers would ever do that to me."

Campbell, leaning against one of two decorative columns at the foot of her bed, let it all roll off him. Chloe had been trying to turn him into Killian or Sawyer his entire life, and he'd been resisting just as long.

"I presume you're referring to China's sister, Janet," Campbell said as she made a selection out of her closet and tossed it on the bed. She paused to look up at him.

"I am," she replied, then walked farther into the wardrobe where her shoes were. She could be in there for hours.

"China said she had to leave a message. Janet could be out of touch for days, maybe longer if she's found someone who is part of her family or someone who knows them. I promised Flamingo Gables I'd be there in a week. I'm going to spend the next few days packing and taking care of things. If and when Janet turns up, I'll get time off."

Chloe emerged a little rumpled, a pair of white pumps in her hand, her expression still severe. "There will be other estate-management jobs."

"I want this one," he said patiently. "It's a smaller house so there's less staff to manage, but it has more grounds. They market citrus fruit and flowers and that's a challenge I'd enjoy."

She threw the shoes on the floor and marched over to face him, a full head shorter than he was. But he'd stood toe-to-toe with her enough times to respect her power and, reluctantly, her wisdom.

"Why must your whole life be all about finding *more?*"

He hated that she didn't get this. "It's not about finding more. It's about finding something different."

"Something that isn't Abbott." It clearly pained her to say the words.

He struggled to edit them correctly. "Something that hasn't already been done better by Killian and Sawyer," he said calmly. "I love them, I love you, I love this place, but I struggle every day to find myself in all this. Killian's smarter, Sawyer's braver, and I don't resent them or need to compete with them, I just need to get out from *behind* them."

"If they stand in front of you," Chloe said, gesticulating so that the blue silk flew, "it is only to protect you. To help you."

"I know that. But I no longer need protection or help. I have to do this."

"And what about me?" she demanded, her expression changing, with a theatrical little sniff, from demanding matriarch to beleaguered victim. "I'm just an old woman trying to hold a volatile family together. And now there's some problem with a customer and Killian may have to go back to England. Sophie wants to take Sawyer to Vermont...."

Campbell stifled a laugh, but withholding a smile over her performance was too much to ask. *"Maman,"* he said, taking hold of her shoulders, "you will never be old, and the rest of you Abbotts are so tightly knit nothing will ever drive you apart. You can wear that pout all you want, but you'll never convince anyone, certainly not me, that you're just a poor little widow woman."

She punched him in the arm. "You would leave China at a time when she struggles to know who *she* is?"

He wondered if his mother had heard anything he'd said. "She doesn't like me. When she finds Janet, they can exchange boxes, and she might—"

Chloe's eyes darkened. "When she read the disappointing news," she pointed out, "she ran into *your* arms."

He remembered that moment. Had, in fact, thought about it much of the night and didn't know what to make of it.

"I was nearby."

"She ignored me and Cordie, who were right beside her, to get to you."

That was true. She had. When he didn't know what to say to that, his mother took advantage of his silence and went on, "Killian and Sawyer tell me that though the two of you quarreled all the time, you managed to work well together. Like true siblings."

"Mom, the test just proved that we're not brother and sister. And just as she has to find her identity, I have to find mine."

"You know you're an Abbott."

"I know my name, Mother. I know my parents and the whole line of my ancestry back to Thomas and Abigail who came over on the *Mayflower*. What I don't know is what I'm capable of. Someone's always trying to protect me from it, or do it for me."

"That isn't true! You think you haven't contributed to a project unless you've done it entirely on your own. You're just like your grandfather Marceau, who tilled fifty acres in Provence all by himself for forty years and finally died of a heart attack."

Campbell frowned at her. "But he did it for forty years."

"Slowly. Had he been willing to pay a little help, he'd have had more time to spend with your grandmother, more time to spend with his children."

"Perhaps he loved all of you very much, but felt compelled to work the soil."

The blue silk flew up again as she expressed her exasperation. "Very well. I'm through trying to persuade you. You'll do as you wish just as you've always done. But mark my words—the day will come when what *you* want will have to come second, and with no experience at putting yourself second, you might not know what to do and lose everything."

"Everything?" His eyebrows rose.

"A woman. Love."

"I have a lot to do before I get serious about a woman."

She smiled at him and shook her head at the same time, negating whatever happy message had been in the smile. "In some ways, you are the most talented of my children. Killian is brilliant in business, and Sawyer can make money dance. But you know so much about so many things, and yet you know so little about yourself."

"That's why I'm going away," he said emphatically, thrilled to finally be able to make his point.

She sighed and shook her head again, as though he was a particularly thickheaded child. "You don't even know where to find yourself."

That cryptic message delivered, she shooed him toward the door. "Go. Cordie and Sophie and I are going shopping for wedding dresses." At the door, she caught his arm. "You will find time to come home for your brother's wedding?"

He remembered Sophie saying something about Labor Day nuptials. "I will."

"Good. If all goes well, Abigail will be home for it, too. Perhaps you can stay long enough to apologize for not letting her play with your dump truck." She pushed him out into the hall and closed the door on him.

He let his forehead fall against it. This family was hopeless. They loved you with a loyalty that was ferocious, but if you didn't adhere completely to the family line, you were badgered until you came "to your senses."

He headed for the stairs, intending to grab something to eat in the kitchen and head for the orchard. Maybe the physical labor of apple-picking would help clear his head.

He found Cordie and Sophie at the table in the kitchen poring over a baby-furniture catalog. Kezia stood behind them. All three looked up expectantly as he walked in.

Dressed for shopping in the city, his brothers' ladies were quite a picture. There had always been women around the house, but with Cordie and Sophie, Shepherd's Knoll had a whole new atmosphere, one that included feminine giggling, too-loud rhythm and blues on the sound system, and more trails of perfume.

"Did she talk you into staying?" Sophie asked hopefully.

"He has to go," Cordie replied before he could, the words intended to convey support for his stand on self-discovery. But he knew she wanted him to stay as much as Killian did. "He needs more scope than we provide," she went on with a graceful wave of her hand. "Life on a bigger canvas, more depth and drama…"

He crossed to the table, caught the hand with which she gestured and kissed her knuckles. "There is no more drama anywhere, Cordelia," he said, "than that which you provide." She'd been a model, done marketing for her father's furniture-manufacturing company, and buying for Abbott Mills. She was red-haired and unflaggingly cheerful, and had driven Killian to distraction.

But now, with twins on the way, she and Killian were ecstatically happy.

"Why are you looking at baby furniture?" he asked, going to the refrigerator. "I thought you were wedding-dress shopping."

"We're going to do both."

He wondered why China wasn't with them. The women had done a lot together since Cordie and Killian had come home from Europe, where they'd had a second honeymoon and checked on the Abbott Mills London office.

"We invited China," Sophie said, "but she insisted she had work to do."

"I think she's going to try to keep her distance until her sister comes." Cordie weighed in with that opinion. "She thinks because she isn't an Abbott, she's lost the right to hang around with us. You could explain to her that that isn't true."

He turned away from the open refrigerator. "Why don't you explain it to her? You're the ones she isn't hanging around with."

"Whose arms did she run into when she learned she wasn't an Abbott?" Cordie asked significantly.

He turned back to the refrigerator. "I was closest."

"No, you weren't."

"What *are* you looking for?" Kezia came to peer over his shoulder. "I can make you bacon and eggs, an omelet, French toast."

"I was looking for the leftover peach pie from last night."

"For breakfast?"

"Peach is a fruit," he said, spotting the pie in the back on the bottom shelf and reaching in for it. "Crust is flour and water and butter. It's just like having toast, only better-tasting."

Kezia made a sound that suggested pain. "Please let me make you something nourishing."

"This'll be great." He took the fairly large slice left on the pie tin, wrapped one end in a paper towel and took off for the orchard with a parting wave for the women, encouraging them to have fun.

He heard Cordie say feelingly, "That's one bad Abbott."

FROM BETWEEN the apple-laden branches of the Duchess, China saw Campbell striding toward the orchard. The Duchess was a large, old tree, part of a group of vintage trees at the end of the orchard. They were the legacy of a colonist who'd owned the property just after the American Revolution. According to local lore, he'd visited his friend, Thomas Jefferson, and brought home thirty-five Esopus Spitzenburg apple trees because he'd so enjoyed the fruit at Jefferson's table.

Twenty-six of the trees had survived thanks to the tireless efforts of the Abbotts.

The family's larger, commercial orchard was populated with Northern Spy apples, but family and friends preferred the "Spitz" for its crisp, sweet taste.

She'd come out this morning to continue to thin the developing crop so that the remaining fruit would have the chance to develop more fully, a process she'd been helping Campbell with for several days. Because of the age of the trees, he preferred to do the work himself, rather than leave it to the occasional staff that helped with the big orchard.

It amazed her to think that just a month ago she hadn't even thought about apples having a history, and now she was blown away by the notion that Thomas Jefferson has probably touched this tree.

It saddened her to know that her days here were numbered, but she'd awakened today, determined to make the most of whatever time she had left at Shepherd's Knoll. She'd also resolved to stop fighting with Campbell. She'd thought about it most of the sleepless night, and couldn't imagine why she'd run into his arms last night after reading the DNA lab report. She could still see everyone's shocked faces. Curiously, Campbell had been the only one who hadn't seemed surprised.

She didn't like him. He didn't like her. Possibly he was willing to offer comfort because he was relieved she wasn't his sister; he felt he could afford to be generous.

But what had prompted *her* to go to *him?* Some need to resolve things with him, maybe, because she knew her little fantasy of being an Abbott was over?

It didn't really matter, she thought, working the shears carefully. She was going to be polite and productive, and pretty soon she would hear from Janet, tell her to come to Losthampton on the next available flight, and then when she was sure Janet was Abigail Abbott, she, China, would be free to go.

She didn't want to infringe upon Janet's right to assume her real life, nor on the Abbotts' hospitality. They might try to talk her into staying, and Janet would probably remind her of their vow that they were sisters no matter what and that gave China some right to be here, but she wouldn't stay. For she was part of whatever life

Janet was discovering at this very moment somewhere in the northern Canadian wilderness. Poor shopping there, she imagined.

Campbell, in jeans and a dark blue T-shirt, came to stand under the Duchess. She smiled pleasantly at him to implement her new plan. Unfortunately she wasn't watching what she was doing and dropped a small, hard-culled apple on his head. Or she would have if he hadn't dodged it.

"You don't have to do this today," he said, steadying the ladder as she reached for a cull.

"This is your last chance to have someone else help you with the picking," she said. "You should take advantage of it."

"I'm leaving before you are. In a few days this is going to be someone else's responsibility."

She glanced down at him in surprise. "You're leaving before Janet comes?"

"I had promised to report for work at the end of the week. And right now, you're not sure where your sister is. I'll come back to meet her when she arrives."

"Who's going to replace you?"

"Everyone's hoping *you* are."

Distracted again, she chipped her fingernail with the shears.

"It wouldn't be fair," she said. "This is another woman's life. Maybe Janet's."

"Don't we all live in each other's lives?"

It was interesting, she thought, that though they didn't get along at all, he was able to pinpoint the one thing in all this she was having difficulty letting go.

When she'd set out on this journey to find out if she was Abigail Abbott, it was because she'd wanted to find the life that was really hers. True, she'd loved her adopted parents, and Janet couldn't be more her sister than if they'd been born twins. But since she'd been aware of what adoption meant, she'd felt a burning desire, if not a desperate need, to know about her past. She couldn't explain it.

And whoever had given her life had bequeathed her a possessiveness and a single-mindedness that often made her difficult to live with.

"Come down from there," he said, tugging at her pant leg, "before you cut off your finger."

Even *she* thought stopping was a good idea. She handed down the shears. "You're right about living in each other's lives," she said when she had reached solid ground. She helped him fold the ladder. "But aren't you the one who has to leave here to find the place where you belong? And you were born to Chloe. Your brothers are your blood. What is it *you* need to know?"

He laughed lightly, self-effacingly. "I guess I'm proof that blood isn't always what it's all about. It's about feeling that you fit in, that you do your share, that your contributions are valuable and significant." He grinned now, his expression ripe with all the unpleasant words that had passed between them since her arrival. "Much as it pains me to admit it," he conceded grudgingly, "your time spent here has been all that."

She couldn't believe her ears, and made a production of slapping a hand against the side of her head as though something obstructed her hearing. "You didn't just say

I've worked hard and well?" she asked in a theatrically shocked voice as they picked up opposite ends of the ladder and carried it to the toolshed. "Because I don't think I could survive a compliment from you. I've been so changed by all your criticisms and complaints that I survive on them. A kind word would—"

"Give it a rest," he advised, pointing to the shed's closed door. "Would you open it, please?"

She held the door open, putting her wrist to the back of her forehead as he walked past her and inside. "I'm feeling faint," she went on. "Everything's beginning to blur. The whole—"

He stood the ladder up and leaned it into its spot in the corner, then took the shears from his belt and placed them on the tool bench. She'd followed him inside. "Put a sock in it, China. Your work's been good, but your mouth and your attitude have been a big problem for me."

"Probably because you have the same mouth, the same attitude."

They looked into each other's eyes under the harsh fluorescent light, the smells of herbal supplements, natural pesticides and the oil that kept the equipment running permeating the air. She had that sense again of being somewhere that would have been so foreign to her just a month ago.

As this man would have been. Though dressed for physical labor, Campbell had the Abbott breeding and grace so apparent in Killian's and Sawyer's good manners and kindness. Until now she'd found it less visible in Campbell, because she'd always been focused on how difficult he was and how angry he made her, but though they'd exchanged little barbs this morning, some subtle change was taking place in the way they dealt with each other.

His treatment of her didn't offend her quite so much now that she knew he *wasn't* her brother, and he seemed a little more inclined to pull his punches—maybe for the same reason.

"If there's a brother in your real life," he speculated, taking her elbow in an unconscious gesture and pushing her ahead of him toward the door, "he may be harder to get along with than I've been."

While he padlocked the door, she walked out into the sunshine, aware of a persistent prickling on her arm. She rubbed at it. "I don't know if that's possible," she teased. "In any case, I'll be well prepared."

"Something bite you?" he asked, indicating the arm she chafed.

"I don't know." She twisted her arm awkwardly to look at it. "It just sort of…"

"Let me see." He took hold of her arm and leaned down to study it more closely. "There're spiders in the shed. Not that they'd mistake you for something sweet."

"Ha-ha." The artificial laugh came out breathy and surprised, instead of as the taunting response she'd intended. And as the air left her lungs, she understood the reason for the new tingle on her arm.

His touch!

The tingle ran from her shoulder to her elbow now as his fingertips traced a path there, looking for the source of the problem. Then it trickled down her wrist as he explored further.

"I don't see anything," he said finally, running his thumb over the back of her elbow one last time.

The tingle followed the path of his thumb. Against every ounce of willpower she tried to muster, heat rose from her throat and crept into her cheeks.

She saw him take note, watched his eyes linger on her blushing face, his expression changing from momentary confusion to something she didn't even want to analyze.

She snatched her arm away. "I must have scraped it on the door," she said quickly. I…I've got to get back to the house. I promised I'd go wedding-dress shopping with the girls and I have to shower."

He opened his mouth to speak, but she didn't wait to hear. She ran for the house and into the kitchen, where Sophie and Cordie still sat.

"Oh, good!" she said breathlessly. "You haven't left yet."

Cordie studied her worriedly. "What's the matter? What happened?"

"Nothing. Can I change my mind and come with you?"

Sophie nodded. "We're still waiting for Chloe. She's having trouble finding a comfortable pair of shoes."

Thank goodness. China abhorred the thought of being left alone here alone with Campbell.

"I can be showered and dressed in twenty minutes," she promised.

Cordie smiled. "Take thirty. We might still be waiting for Chloe."

China took thirty, but the tingle would not wash off no matter how hard she scrubbed. Campbell's touch was invisibly tattooed on her arm. She didn't want to think about what that might mean.

Well, she told herself practically as she pulled on white slacks and a white cotton blouse. It could mean whatever she wanted it to mean. She was in charge of her own destiny. Reaction to a man's touch did not have to mean attraction. The touch of *any* polite and presentable man might have done that to her. It was a physical response, nothing more.

She repeated that to herself as she brushed her unruly hair and pinned it into a neat knot at the back of her head. But her cheeks filled with color again as she remembered the moment.

She put both hands to her eyes and groaned. No. Please, no. She could not be attracted to Campbell Abbott.

She'd thought he was her brother, and she'd disliked him intensely. Now that she was almost free to leave here, she wanted nothing to get in her way.

But that, she remembered, was what he did best.

Chapter Three

Campbell transferred the contents of his desk into a box—a box, he noticed, that looked a lot like the one with which China had arrived on their doorstep.

He fell into his desk chair, wishing that thought hadn't occurred to him. It reminded him of the terrible tension of the whole month she'd been here and the possible reason for it that was just beginning to surface.

He kept packing, refusing to let the idea form. No, no no. He was reporting to Flamingo Gables next Friday as he'd promised, and nothing or no one was going to stop him.

It was his chance—finally—to live life on his own terms and he wasn't going to give up that chance because a woman had blushed when he'd touched her. A woman he'd thought until last night might be his sister. A woman who disliked him.

That was it. They were all victims of the emotional riot of the DNA report, the anticipation of it and the disappointment with the results of it. China Grant wasn't attracted to him. She was so upset she barely knew her own name right now.

And he wasn't attracted to her. She was too mouthy, too opinionated, too quick to say what she thought regardless of the consequences.

While he might have admired those qualities in any other woman, they were too much like his own bad habits to allow for coexistence within the same family. Of course, now they weren't *in* the same family.

"Hey." Killian walked into his office with several more empty boxes. He looked around at the stacks of things on the floor and asked in mild concern, "Is this progress or chaos?"

"I guess life is always a little of both." Campbell replied, emptying the stationery in the last desk drawer into the box. He folded the flaps and wrote "Office" on the lid.

Killian came to sit on the edge of his desk. "That's pretty philosophical for you. You usually just storm ahead without giving things too much thought."

"Thinking complicates things." Campbell carried the box to the wall near the door where others were stacked. "It's best to go with gut instinct."

Killian watched him walk to a pile of books and pick out a sturdy box to put them in. "What's the matter?" Killian asked in the neutral voice that meant he was trying to sound interested, not like an authority figure. "There seems to be a new desperation in your eagerness to leave."

Campbell looked up at him with deliberate innocence. "No. You're just being paternal again. Reading things into the situation that aren't there."

"Okay." Killian raised both hands in a backing-off gesture. "We'll just presume that you know what you're doing."

"Let's."

"If it's not challenging your autonomy too much, can you reassure me that you have a plan in place for the apple harvest since you won't be here?"

Campbell stopped packing to go back to the desk, guilt plaguing him that Killian even had to ask the question. Campbell was the estate manager, after all. If the manager had been anyone else, he'd have had to present a plan in writing long before he was ready to leave.

"Of course I do," he assured him quietly. "Robby Thompson from Lake Grove—he always heads up the harvest hiring—has been involved with me enough times to handle it himself. He's good with the workers and he has a good sense of when work's done quickly and well. And I've left him a step-by-step, just in case."

Killian stood, apparently satisfied. "I figured you had," he said. "I just wanted to hear it for certain. Things have been a little weird for all of us lately."

Weird. To be sure.

"Mom says you may have to go back to London." Campbell followed Killian to the door, hating the way his half brother hovered but somehow needing him to stay a minute longer.

Killian stopped in the doorway. "Yeah. Customer Relations has asked me to come back. They're dealing with a disgruntled customer who represents about forty percent of our sales in Europe. I'm leaving day after tomorrow. I hate to miss the last couple of days you're home, but I have to be there."

Campbell understood that. "Sure. You taking Cordie?"

Killian smiled, revealing a tender vulnerability Campbell wasn't used to seeing in his face. "I don't want her out of my sight before she delivers."

"Good thinking. Well, what about if I take you and Sawyer to dinner tomorrow night? Fulio's?"

"I think Mom's planning a family thing at home the night before I leave."

News of that plan had leaked when he'd overheard his mother on the phone. "Yeah. But I was thinking the three of us should get out together before I go."

"Ah…sure. Sounds good to me. I know Sawyer's free because the girls at Abbott's West are having a baby shower for Cordie." Cordie had worked as the buyer for the women's wear department of the Abbott's West store. "Mom, Sophie and Kezia are all going."

"Perfect timing. Should we include Daniel?"

"Sure."

"Brian, too?"

"Why not?" Brian was Killian and Sawyer's newly discovered half brother, the result of Susannah Stewart Abbott's affair with Corbin Girard, their married neighbor and the man behind the November Corporation, the arch business enemy of Abbott Mills.

Killian studied Campbell one last time. "You're sure you're okay about leaving? No plan suffers from rethinking it."

This one would, Campbell thought. He nodded. "I'm good. So, six o'clock tomorrow we'll head out, okay?"

"Okay. You want me to tell Sawyer and Daniel?"

"Sure. That'd help."

"All right." Killian pointed to the still-incomplete stack of boxes. "You shipping all this or are you driving down?"

"Driving. I'm shipping some of it. Don't worry, okay? I've got everything under control."

"Right." Killian slapped him on the shoulder. "Later."

There was something strangely unnerving about standing alone amid the disassembled pieces of his business life in the house where he'd spent the past thirty-one years. While this was exactly what he wanted—a life apart from the family so that he could see where he fit—now that it came to it, he felt the pull of its comfort and security as he never had before.

Though he loved and respected his half brothers, he'd always been jealous that they'd come first, that they'd been part of his father's life before he had, and that his mother, who was their stepmother, loved them every bit as much as she loved him.

Whenever Chloe had wanted better behavior from him, she'd talk about Killian's fine qualities, Sawyer's good nature. But Campbell had been born—as Chloe claimed—with his grandfather's seriousness and tendency to do what he wanted without consultation. That wasn't a good quality, she'd said, for success in family relationships.

Rather than strive to be more like his older siblings, he'd taken pride in being as unlike them as possible. Their father had died when he was in high school. He'd tried to quit school, tried to run off to the city, but Killian, with Sawyer's support, had dragged him back and made him stay. That episode had both deepened his respect and increased his resentment.

He was so confused about his relationship with his brothers that it was his senior year in college before he forgave them for taking over his life. He'd become a team player as far as anything that involved the family went, but his resistance to whatever his brothers wanted him to do or be had become habit. He loved them, but he wasn't staying. On some level that he couldn't quite explain or even really understand, he didn't belong here.

Weird, he thought as he continued to pack, that he could see China staying more than he could see himself doing so.

THE BRIDAL DEPARTMENT of Abbott's West on Manhattan's Upper West Side was another place China would have never expected to find herself just a month ago. The new buyer for the department was obviously eager to help Cordie—the boss's wife—and Sophie find the perfect dress. Tina Bishop was a leggy blonde with very short hair that complemented her fine-featured face and big blue eyes. These eyes studied Sophie, then the other three. She disappeared into the back of the store.

She came back with three dresses wrapped in plastic sleeves draped carefully across her arms. She hung them on a hook near the mirrors as China and her companions crowded closer.

"You should show off that waistline," Tina advised, pulling the wrapper off the first to reveal an ivory affair with a beaded bodice, long sleeves and a billowy floor-length chiffon skirt.

Sophie grimaced. "It's lovely," she said apologetically, "but I was thinking of something much less… fussy. This is a second wedding for me and I'm hardly a girl any—"

"What?" Cordie swatted Sophie's arm. "Have you been in the hospital's drug cabinet?" Sophie was an ER nurse at Losthampton Hospital. "You're not getting married in a gray suit, and that's final."

Sophie swatted her back. "That wasn't my intention. I just don't think lots of chiffon and heavy beading is called for. I'm hardly—"

"If you say you're hardly a girl," Chloe interrupted, "I'll be forced to swat you, too."

Tina caught China's eye and grinned as the Abbott women squabbled. "In effect," Tina said, "this is their store, so I have little choice but to let them duke it out. Do you know what style she had in mind for you bridesmaids? What color?"

China shook her head, even as she felt the stirrings of an idea. "I imagine you carry Lauren Llewellyn?"

Tina visibly warmed at the mention of the designer's name. "She deals exclusively with the Abbott stores in the city."

China drew the buyer slightly away from the still-quarreling group. "I'm a personal shopper in Los Angeles, and I recently helped a wedding planner in Belmont Shores find the dresses for the bride and her party from Lauren Llewellyn's fall collection. It was very thirties. The Gatsby Girls, I think she called it. Are you familiar…?"

Tina was nodding before China could even finish. "You're right. But there was no wedding dress, as I recall."

"No, but there was an ivory tea-length dress with a wide, ruffled…"

Tina snapped her fingers and disappeared.

Chloe, Cordie and Sophie stopped arguing and turned to China in alarm.

"What happened?" Cordie asked. "Where did she go?"

China sat on a powder-blue banquette that faced the mirrors. "To call the police, I think. Something about it being store policy when patrons come to blows and it's pretty clear there's not going to be a sale involved…"

Three flushed faces frowned at her.

She smiled. "Okay, she went to get another dress. Perhaps if we all sit down and behave ourselves, she'll show it to us."

They collected around China on the long sofa, Cordie frowning at her teasingly. "You sound just like an Abbott."

China laughed. It wasn't really funny, but she had to get over the sadness of it. "Well, now that I know I'm not one, I can push you around without fear of retribution."

Chloe leaned toward her with mock seriousness. "You must always fear me, *ma chère.* And you *are* family whether you want to be or not. Just like Campbell."

Tina was back in a few minutes with the very dress China had in mind. A rich ivory chiffon, it had a draped neckline and split flutter sleeves. Sophie gasped as Tina held up the hanger and splayed the tea-length, asymmetrical hem of the skirt over her other arm.

"It's perfect," Sophie breathed.

"Llewellyn is the finest ready-to-wear designer working today," Tina said. "Before you try it on, would you like to see what she has in mind for your bridesmaids?"

"She?" Sophie asked, then turned to Tina as she gestured at China. "How did you know about this dress, China?"

"I'm a personal shopper at home," she replied, then explained about the Belmont Shores wedding. "The bride had the wedding planner at her wits' end. She was a friend of mine, and I happened to remember seeing the dresses in Llewellyn's fall collection."

Tina put the ivory dress on the hook, then returned with a dress of similar cut, with the same neckline and sleeves, but with a diagonal ruffle that ran from hip to knee and matched the asymmetrical hem. It was also chiffon.

"It's perfect!" Cordie said, touching the ruffle. "What colors does it come in?"

"We have it in jade, persimmon, dusk and dawn. Dusk is a sort of purply-blue, and dawn is pink to dark lavender. If you want the two in different colors, I'd say dusk and dawn. Dusk for Cordie. It'll be perfect with your hair."

"Go!" Chloe ordered. "Go try them on while Tina helps me find something for the mother of the bride."

"Mom," Cordie said, "you're the mother of the groom."

Chloe shrugged. "Her mother isn't here, so I am mother of the entire wedding. Go!"

Cordie, Sophie and China disappeared obediently into the fitting rooms with the dresses Tina brought them.

China shucked her Long Island whites and pulled the filmy fabric on over her head. She cursed Kezia's good cooking when she had to wriggle through the snug-fitting lining of the bodice. She avoided the mirror as she tugged the also-snug skirt down over her hips and let the bias-cut folds of fabric fall to just above her ankles.

She could plead for a looser style, she thought, which would probably be better for Cordie, anyway. Or some kind of filmy tunic to cover…

She turned to the mirror, wincing against what she was going to see…then decided quickly her reflection wasn't bad at all. She didn't have Sophie's ethereal good looks, maybe, or Cordie's ebullience, which made her look good in anything.

But apparently all the physical labor she'd done in the orchard had countered the extra calories she'd consumed at the table. The fabric clung to her breasts, her rib cage, her waist and her hips, and—if she sucked in her breath—was even flattering. The skirt rippled around her slender ankles as she kicked off her comfortable slip-ons and stood on tiptoe to see where the hemline would fall when she wore heels.

"How do you look?" Sophie's voice shouted over the tops of the roofless dressing rooms. "I'm quite gorgeous!"

"Me, too!" Cordie said from the room in between. "Well, except for my belly."

"Pregnant bellies are gorgeous," Sophie called, sounding euphoric. "You won't believe how perfect this dress is!"

"I'm sure it's because you're in it. China?"

"Yeah?"

"Are you gorgeous?"

"Ah...well, passable, anyway. But I'm going to need control-top panty hose."

Cordie giggled. "I wish that could help me."

"I'm coming out," Sophie said. "Meet you at the mirrors."

Her fitting-room door opened and closed, and China remained rooted to the spot, still looking at her reflection in amazement. She was the same woman she'd been when she arrived at Shepherd's Knoll, but the experience of almost having and then losing a wonderful prize showed in her face. She didn't look sad, precisely, just a little...misplaced. Uncertain. Longing. Fortunately, when she walked out of the fitting room and toward the mirrors, the fabric floating around her legs, Cordie and Sophie didn't see any of that.

"You look beautiful!" Cordie said, walking around her, then looking over her shoulder in the mirror. "Wow. I can't believe how right you were about these dresses. Look at Sophie!"

Sophie did a turn in front of the three-way, a small dancing army in ruffly ivory reflected back at them. The cut was perfect for her graceful slenderness, and she glowed with the confidence of wearing a garment she knew made the most of her figure and her personality. She spun away from the mirror to face them, her eyes aglow.

"You can't leave Shepherd's Knoll," she said to China. "You have to do my clothes shopping all the time."

Cordie went to the mirror, turned sideways and held a hand under her round little stomach. She wasn't very big yet, but big enough that her curves played havoc with the straight lines of the dress, yet were somewhat camouflaged by the diagonal ruffle. She wound up her long red ponytail and held it to the back of her head.

"Helps the line a little, don't you think?"

Sophie and China flanked her, Sophie doing the same with her long hair. "I think we could go on the road with a sister act," Sophie said.

"Except that we aren't sisters and we can't sing," China said.

"Sisters-in-law are close enough." Cordie put an arm around Sophie's shoulders. "You're the one putting a damper on everything. If you'd marry Campbell, we could have very profitable careers."

"Campbell and I hate each other," China said, knowing even as the words came out of her mouth that that was now mysteriously untrue. At least, not true to the degree it had once been. "And who needs a profitable career when you're an Abbott?"

Sophie's reflection raised an eyebrow at hers. "What about our emotional need to perform? To watch the curtain rise, hear the audience applaud?"

"That wouldn't happen. We can't sing."

"How do we know?" Sophie persisted. "What if our three dissonant voices came together to make the perfect sound? We'll never know, will we, because you're selfishly leaving us."

"Not until her sister arrives," Cordie reminded the bride-to-be. "There's still time to change her mind. Does your sister sing, China?"

The silliness went on.

Then Chloe came out of the fitting room in a skirt

similar in style to theirs but with a more tailored jacket, the irregular length of its hem its only concession to the thirties style. The color was somewhere between China's pink lavender and Cordie's purply blue. It was sensational with her gray hair and fair complexion.

She slipped in under China's arm to become part of the chorus-girl lineup. Playfully, she pointed her toe and showed some leg.

"That's it!" Sophie said. "Even if we can't sing, we can dance!"

"Oh, I'd be graceful," Cordie said dryly, and broke away.

Chloe groaned. "I suffer from arthritis."

"I suffer from two left feet." China followed her cohorts toward the dressing room.

Sophie sighed and fell into line behind them. "It's tough being a visionary when you're among a bunch of dullards," she complained.

Chapter Four

"I don't understand what just happened," Sawyer said, turning to Campbell in mystification. He, Campbell and Killian sat across from Cordie, Sophie and China at the game table in one of the family rooms. "What do you mean, queens are wild? I've never heard of queens being wild in rummy. I have three aces."

"They're not worth anything in 'millionaire rummy,'" China replied, gathering up their cards. She was dealer.

Campbell watched her serious expression, waiting for it to crack. So far, through the "deuces double the value of tens" rule, the "highest score gets a fifty-point penalty" rule, and the "first one to get a royal flush wins" rule, it was flawless. "I've never heard of millionaire rummy before tonight," he said.

"Me, neither," his brothers chorused.

China gazed at each of them in innocent disbelief, her eyes landing barely a second on him. "And each of you a millionaire. Go figure."

"Queens Are Wild is our stage name," Sophie said,

as she stood up to reach the coffee carafe in the middle of the table and began topping up everyone's cup.

"Stage name?" Sawyer gaped.

She nodded. "We're going on the road as a song-and-dance team."

Killian said to Cordie with exaggerated gentleness, "Sweetheart, you can't sing."

She shrugged that off as she held out her cup. "Our dancing will cover that. Show a little leg and the crowd will go wild. No one will hear our sour notes over the cheering."

Sawyer turned to Killian, his expression half amused, half worried. He turned back to the women. "What happened out there today?"

"Don't you see it?" Killian asked, taking a sip from his cup. "They went dress shopping and discovered they have chemistry. They're intending to take over the world with it, starting with a simple card game."

"Ah. Well, that'll have to wait until Sophie and I return from Vermont, and Killian and Cordie are finished in London. Unless China chooses to strike out on her own, just to warm up your potential audience."

"Oh, I don't think so." Sophie sounded discouraged. "She's convinced that talent is all-important. And as she keeps reminding us, she's not a sister."

"But neither are you and Cordie."

"We're sisters-in-law. Or will be. Close enough."

"Well, there you go." Killian took Campbell's cup and held it up for Cordie to refill. "You have to marry China to save their musical careers. Then she'll be a sister, and she can still perform while Cordie and Sophie are away."

"And that helps you and Sawyer and me how?" Campbell asked.

Killian handed back his cup. "They become stars, support us in the manner to which we are accustomed, and the three of us kick back and…I don't know, race Brian's boats, or Sawyer can teach us to do stunts on motorcycles. We can have fun for a change."

Killian had spun out the whole scenario simply to carry on the joke, but Campbell thought it was interesting to hear his workaholic brother talk about having fun. His refusal to allow himself to enjoy anything—a legacy of the guilt all the brothers shared over Abby's kidnapping—had been part of the reason for his initial breakup with Cordie. Their reconciliation and the pending arrival of their babies had helped him loosen up, lighten up.

China, on the other hand, had pushed back her chair, taken the empty cookie plate into the kitchen and returned with it full again. She reached over Sawyer to put it in the middle of the table.

"Thanks, China." Sawyer patted her hand. "I think she'd make a great sister-in-law," he said, glancing at the other two women. "It didn't occur to either of you to refill the cookie plate."

"If she married me," Campbell teased, watching her face for a change of expression, "she'd be moving with me to Flamingo Gables, and that wouldn't help your quest for cookies, anyway. Or the whole sister-act plan. She'd be a thousand miles away."

"If I married you," China corrected, no betrayal of discomfort in her eyes, though there was a little color in her cheeks, "you'd be coming with me to Canada's far north to find my family."

For one quick moment, unconnected with the here and now, he speculated on what it would be like to follow her to the Canadian north. He got a mental image of moose and bear, pine trees, snow-covered hills and a snug log cabin with a fire going inside. There was furniture upholstered in plaid wool, a big bed covered with a thick quilt—and the two of them in it. Her search wasn't going well and she was crying just as she had the night she'd opened the report from the lab. But now she was naked in his arms, pressed to him for comfort, arms wrapped around him. He could feel the soft inside of her leg hitched over his thigh, her pearled breasts against his chest. The image was very real and it shook him to the bone.

"Campbell? Cam!" Killian's voice.

Campbell came back to the moment to find everyone around the table watching him in concern. Had he said something? he wondered. Groaned? He looked across the table at China and saw that she was as perplexed as the rest of them. Odd, considering how real those images had been, that she didn't remember inhabiting them.

"Yeah?" he asked.

"I said that I spoke to Brian about checking in at the house every couple of days while we're all away," Killian repeated patiently. "And being available to Winfield if he needs him."

"Why would your butler-cum-security-force need Brian?" Sophie asked.

"Sometimes when he's worried about Mom's safety

and does or doesn't want her to do something, he needs support from one of us to get her cooperation."

"And you'll all be available to come right back," China asked, "if Janet suddenly calls?"

Killian nodded. "We're just an overnight flight away."

"And we'll be close enough to drive home in a few hours," Sawyer said.

"What about you, Campbell?" China challenged with a smile. Mentally, he had to put clothes back on her. The tips of her breasts were driving him crazy. "How are you going to get away when you'll be so new on the job?"

He pushed away from the table, returning her polite smile. "My employer's prepared. I explained when I accepted the job that there was a family complication. Of course, at the time I thought it was you."

As the words left his mouth, he realized that he'd called her a complication. His hope that no one had noticed was dashed when Killian gave him a raised eyebrow. China, however, took it with a lift of her chin and a go-to-hell glance. "I always thought *you* were the complicated one," she said.

He stood and pushed his chair in. "If you'll all excuse me, I've got to pay some bills tonight so the household accounts are all caught up when I leave. And don't forget tomorrow night."

Sawyer's brow furrowed. "Tomorrow night?"

Killian groaned. "Sorry, Cam. I forgot to tell him. And I'm supposed to be the smart one."

Campbell snorted and addressed Sawyer. "I'm taking you, Killian, Brian and Daniel to dinner at Fulio's while the ladies are at Cordie's baby shower."

Sawyer put a hand to his heart in a dramatic portrayal of an attack. "What? You mean you're *choosing* to be with us? Even treating us?"

"Only because I won't have to see you for some time afterward. Six o'clock. Be ready."

"Ah…wait. I'm happy to have Daniel with us, but I thought he was driving the girls to the shower. I'm not wild about the idea of them trying to get around in the city."

"I'm driving," China said. "I fight the freeways in L.A. I assure you we'll be safe."

"But you know L.A.," Sawyer argued. "You don't know New York."

"The shower's not in the city," Cordie put in. "It's in Westbury on the west end of the island. And I'll be navigating."

"Oh, God!" Killian exclaimed. "They'll be in Nebraska by morning. We need a plan B."

Cordie walked around the table to pummel him. Laughing, he pulled her into his lap. "All right, all right," he said, holding her fists in one hand. "I'm just remembering the time you were supposed to navigate us to the Dawsons' open house and we ended up in a creek."

"We'll let China use the tractor," Campbell proposed with a straight face. "She drives it quite well, and can mow down anything in her path."

"Does it have global positioning?" Sawyer asked.

Campbell excused himself again and left the room, the laughter still going on. The coziness was beginning to get to him. Life with his brothers had been one thing when Killian had been a workaholic and Sawyer had been determined to kill himself. He'd been able to hold his practical, no-nonsense approach to life up against their baggage and feel somewhat superior.

He couldn't do that anymore.

And it had been easy to plan to leave when the house had been always quiet. In those days, Killian seldom came home from the city, even on weekends, and though Sawyer was home, he kept to himself a lot, working on the foundation's projects and other charitable community functions. Chloe had a busy social life and came and went all the time. The staff was like family, but they were all good employees and worked hard.

So Campbell had spent a lot of time alone, and he'd thought he'd liked it that way—though he'd been determined to spend it alone someplace else. But now that the house was full of women, children, laughter and plans, he felt as though the place had a grip on him and didn't want to let go.

"Uncle Cam!"

That, too, was something new. He turned to see Sophie's two youngest racing toward him from the family room down the hall where they'd gone to watch movies after dinner. Their older sister, Gracie, was staying the night at a friend's.

"What's going on?" he asked, leaning down to catch them in his arms.

"We're going to have a wedding!" Emma said, dark eyes bright at the prospect. "And we're all going to wear pretty dresses and flowers!"

"Oh, no!" he exclaimed. "I don't have a pretty dress!"

She giggled and tugged on his hand. "You're not

gonna wear a dress, silly! Just the ladies wear dresses. You have to wear a special suit."

"A tux." Eddie made a face. "Me, too. I'm going to carry the rings. I hate tuxes."

Eddie was lively and imaginative, and Campbell thought he'd make a great Abbott. "Why?"

"Because I'll look stupid."

"I don't think you will, but if it's any comfort, all of us guys will be wearing tuxes, so you won't be alone."

"When are you going away?" Emma asked.

"Saturday," he replied.

"Sawyer says we're going to come and see you."

"That would be very nice."

"And Grandma Chloe's gonna have a big party for you before you go. And we get to come. On Friday."

"Right."

"It's too bad," Eddie said gravely, "that China isn't Abigail. We really like her." Since their mother's involvement with Sawyer, the children knew all about the family's search for their missing member, understood why China had come to visit.

Campbell nodded, suddenly a little short of breath, out of words. He had to think, clear his throat. "Yes. We all like her. But it could be that the adopted sister she grew up with might be Abigail. Do you know what 'adopted' is?"

"It's when you don't have a mom and dad," Emma put in knowledgeably, "and somebody else's mom and dad let you live with them."

"You have to go to court to be adopted," Eddie said. "And the judge makes your name the same as the new mom and dad's name. One time when we went to court, there was this kid there who was getting adopted. I remember wishing we could get adopted by another dad, only, Mom could come with us. But the court doesn't ever do that."

"Because moms don't get adopted by dads," Emma explained to Eddie, pleased to know something he didn't. "They have to marry them. Like Mom and Sawyer and the wedding."

Eddie rolled his eyes. "I know that. I just meant, that day we were in court, it seemed like it would be a really good idea if it worked that way."

Sophie had had an abusive husband, and the children had seen and experienced things that shouldn't be part of any child's memories.

"Well, it's a good thing that didn't happen," Campbell told him, "because if you'd been given to someone else, you wouldn't be *my* niece and nephew."

Winfield suddenly flew out of the family room where the children had been watching movies. Then he spotted them with Campbell and put a hand to his heart in relief. "Thank goodness," he said in his gravelly voice as he came toward them. "I dozed off during the third viewing of *Nemo*. Party breaking up?"

Campbell had hired Winfield a little more than a year ago, concerned about the family's safety. A butler trained in self-defense and security was suddenly a popular new hybrid among household staff. Winfield was Campbell's height but showed the results of years of weight training as a professional boxer. He had thin blond hair, light blue eyes and a nose that had been broken several times. He was flawlessly courteous to household members and guests of Shepherd's Knoll.

Winfield worked hard at keeping the house safe, though his skills hadn't really been tested. A good result of the very fact that he was there, Campbell thought.

"No, I have a few things to do tonight," Campbell replied, "so I had to excuse myself." He ruffled Eddie's hair and kissed Emma's. "I guess I'll see you at the party."

"Come on, kids." Winfield led the children back to the family room. "Campbell has work to do. Let's go raid the kitchen."

There were cheers of approval, and they ran toward the kitchen ahead of the butler.

Campbell changed into comfortable clothes and went down the back stairs to his office off the kitchen. He could hear Winfield and the children rummaging in the cupboards, talking about crackers and peanut butter and Kezia's lemonade.

He pushed his door silently closed and felt a certain relief at this shutting out the rest of the family. Until he went to his desk and discovered he hadn't escaped everyone.

Versace, Cordie's cat, an obese gray Persian-and-something mix, lay sprawled atop the open book in which he kept hard copies of certain accounts he liked to be able to refer to quickly. Sachi, as Cordie called him, had taken some time adjusting to life at Shepherd's Knoll after Cordie had given up her apartment and moved in. He was choosy about his company, too. Apart from Cordie, he liked Kezia, who gave him treats from the kitchen, and Emma, who talked baby talk to him and carried him around in a manner that appeared to choke the life out of him, but of course didn't.

Now the cat was trying to take over Campbell's office. He would lie on one side of Campbell's desk, invariably on something important, and, with eyes narrowed to lazy golden slits, dare Campbell to try to move him.

Campbell let him be. This office was going to be someone else's province in a few days. He sat in the chair, pulled it to the computer and called up the household file and the schedule of accounts payable.

And then to his complete shock, Versace rolled to his feet and before Campbell could react stepped on the keyboard, scrolling up the document several pages in the process, then stepped into his lap—he went to sleep purring like Killian's Jaguar on a long, straight road.

Campbell gasped helplessly.

A moment later there was a rap on the door. Sachi's head snapped up. China walked in, then stopped beside the desk, eyes wide with amazement.

"Killian sent me," she finally said, "to remind you to leave a check for Tante Bijou's new wheelchair. It's supposed to arrive sometime in the next few days." She shook her head at the picture he made with Versace in his lap. "You're even more complicated than I thought. He likes you?"

"Don't sound so surprised," he replied, cautiously stroking the cat's back. Fortunately Sachi continued to purr. "A lot of people do."

"I like you," she said with a taunting grin. "I just don't get you."

"Back at ya. Drive carefully tomorrow."

"I'm a safe driver." She went to the doorway.

For no reason at all came the image of the two of them in that bed in his imaginary cabin. He closed his eyes against it. But since the picture had formed on his brain and not on his cornea, it remained. "Good night, Campbell," he heard her say.

When he opened his eyes again, she was gone, but her image remained.

DINNER AT FULIO'S was never disappointing. The trattoria had steak and seafood on its menu and desserts to die for. The Abbotts had patronized the restaurant for thirty years. Campbell paid the tab while his brothers and Daniel streamed outside.

"We're going to miss you," Fulio said, taking an impression of his credit card and handing it back. "You sure you're going to be happy in that sunny place? No leaves turning, no snow, no relief that spring is finally coming?"

Campbell repeated the argument he'd given Killian for accepting the post. "Girls in bikinis all year long, Fulio. Think about that."

Fulio closed his eyes and put a hand over his heart. "Ah. I see it."

"I'm still a young man."

Fulio grinned, his eyes still closed. "So am I when I think of such things."

Campbell laughed and clapped his shoulder. "I'll be back, and when I am, I'll come and visit over a bottle of wine."

Fulio opened his eyes and shook Campbell's hand. "You do that. Good luck."

Outside, Campbell's companions milled around near the limo. Though they'd taken the Lincoln limousine, Campbell had driven so that Daniel wouldn't feel he'd been invited only because they needed a driver.

"Where to next?" he asked.

Killian glanced at his watch. "It's after ten."

"So what? The women are gone and we can go out on the town."

Daniel laughed. "Kezia wouldn't have let me come if she'd thought we were going out on the town."

"You and Brian," Sawyer said to Campbell, "are the only two here free to *go* out on the town. The rest of us are committed."

"And you'd get in trouble," Brian said, shaking his head in mock woe. "God, I'm glad we aren't you."

Campbell looked at Killian and Sawyer. "You mean you want to go home before midnight? Without even seeing what's going on at Combustible?"

Combustible was a local bar where locals who enjoyed nightlife always ended up before the night was over. When Campbell was in college, Killian once had to bail him out of jail when a fracas at the bar brought the police. The guy Campbell punched out had made a nasty remark about the relationship between the Abbott men and the sheep on the Abbott Mills logo.

Killian shook his head. "I want to be able to hear my cell phone ring. Cordie promised to call me when they start for home."

"Okay." Campbell unlocked the limousine doors with the remote. "Get in. Brian and I'll take you old fogies home, then come back and have some fun."

Campbell drove home. "I can't believe this," he said as he pulled up in front of the French doors that opened into the library. "This was supposed to be our last hurrah. Our final night out as comrades in arms before I walk out of your lives, and you're calling an end to it at ten-twenty!"

"This is our life now," Killian said with sudden gravity. "I have babies on the way, and Sawyer's assumed the responsibility for three children. You're still free to take off to find yourself and celebrate that with a night on the town, but Sawyer and I will never be that unfettered again. It's an irrefutable fact."

It was. And it hit Campbell like a sledge. He'd spent most of his life knowing he had to literally distance himself from Killian and Sawyer to find out what he was capable of, yet he was comfortable with them, and the three of them knew as no one else did what it was like to grieve over the baby sister who had been taken from their midst and to worry every day of their lives about what had happened to her.

"But you are unfettered, so have that night on the town." Killian slid out of the front seat, then leaned in to add with a smile, "And thanks for dinner. It was fun to make a pauper of you with side dishes, desserts and after-dinner aperitifs."

Sawyer clapped his shoulder as he and Brian and Daniel climbed out of the second seat. "Yeah, thanks. I particularly enjoyed my third dessert."

Daniel leaned into the front. "Thank you, Mr. Campbell. I enjoyed not having to drive."

"I'm happy you all had such fun at my expense." Campbell pretended indignation, but he knew they'd had a good time together. Though circumstances had changed their priorities, they remained allied in their love of Shepherd's Knoll and of one another.

Brian climbed into the front, and Campbell drove away. He reached the road that led to the highway to town in one direction or to the beach in the other. He'd been strangely shaken by Killian's reminder that their lives had changed. He hesitated over which direction to take.

"Your heart set on a drink at Combustible?" he asked Brian.

"No." Brian settled down in his seat. "My heart's never set. You thinking about going to the beach?"

"Yeah. I could use another drink, but I'm suddenly not up to the noise."

"Then let's go to the beach. We've got champagne in the back of the limo."

Campbell turned toward the ocean. "That's inspired, Brian."

"I'm a Girard, after all," Brian said, reaching over the back to the chest that held the champagne service. He snatched the bottle and two glasses. "Though my father rues the day I was born. And I have Stewart blood, though my mother abandoned your brothers. I'm made up of two pretty horrible human beings who sprang from gene pools of serious business savvy."

When Killian and Sawyer's mother discovered she was pregnant with Brian, she left Shepherd's Knoll with the chauffeur. Killian had been five and Sawyer, three.

She'd died in childbirth when Brian was born and the chauffeur had called Girard. He'd been in Japan on business, and so the chauffeur had spoken to his wife, instead. When Girard had returned, his wife had already sent for Brian and insisted it was Corbin's responsibility to raise him as their adopted son, fulfilling his duty to the baby while saving the family from scandal.

Brian had learned all this more than a year ago and had kept it to himself. It had all come out at the hospital about a month earlier when Brian had saved Sawyer's life. Sawyer had been rehearsing a skiing stunt for charity that went very wrong when Sawyer leaped a long line-up of barrels strung together. His ski had caught in a rope, slamming him onto the last barrel, where he lay unconscious with his upper body in the water. Brian had been nearby, testing one of the boats he'd just purchased as part of the business, and found himself in the water when the boat proved not to be seaworthy. He'd swum to Sawyer to hold his head out of the water until Cordie and Killian arrived.

Brian had become a part of their lives since then. He was easy to like and seemed surprisingly grounded for a man who'd been an important part of his father's corporation one moment, then disowned the next when he'd helped Killian resist a business move that might have made Abbott Mills susceptible to a hostile takeover by Corbin Girard's November Corporation.

He'd inherited his maternal grandmother's home about a mile from Shepherd's Knoll and bought a small general store and boat-rental operation on the waterfront.

Campbell envied the ease with which Brian seemed to have handled it all. Campbell felt tossed about and plagued by the confusion in his own life—China's arrival, the thought that she might be Abby, the proof that she wasn't…his incomprehensible feelings for her. What Brian had endured was far worse, yet he seemed remarkably sane.

Of course, there was no woman in his life, which probably made a big difference. Though he got along remarkably well with China.

Campbell parked where the road ended. The July night was warm, the breeze off the ocean refreshing. He got out of the car, pulled off his jacket and sat on the hood of the limo. Brian handed him the champagne and the glasses, then sat beside him.

Campbell pulled the foil and the wire off the bottle. "Did you remember the corkscrew?" he asked Brian.

Brian produced it from his pocket.

"You've got to have some Abbott in you," Campbell said. "You're always prepared."

"That's just good Boy Scout training."

"How many Boy Scouts do you know who drink champagne?"

The moonlight caught Brian's grin. "In our circle, a surprising number. I remember one time a bunch of us were left alone in the Athertons' house to work on a project that was going to earn us some badge or other. We decided to raid the liquor cabinet. We couldn't find any hard stuff, but we broke open a bottle of Rothschild. Everyone else hated it, but I liked it."

"You have excellent taste. Here." The cork pried off, Campbell handed him a full glass. It bubbled and hissed.

"You want to drink *to* something?" Brian asked, propping his feet on the bumper. "Or just drink?"

Campbell thought for a moment. He'd just wanted another drink to dull Killian's remark about everything changing. For someone so anxious to get away, he was inexplicably concerned about how things would be at Shepherd's Knoll when he was gone.

But the night was warm and fragrant, he had a newly discovered brother beside him, and a deep appreciation for his relationship with the men he'd dropped off at the house. Life might be changing, but it was good. Only one matter remained unresolved.

"To finding Abigail," he said, raising his glass to the night.

Brian lifted his glass and repeated the words. They drank.

"Did China tell you anything about her sister?" Brian asked.

"Just that everybody loves her."

Brian laughed lightly. "Sounds like an Abbott. Even the difficult ones." He cast Campbell a wry glance, leaving little doubt as to which of the Abbotts he referred to.

Campbell rose halfheartedly to his own defense. "I'm not difficult. I'm…yeah, I guess I'm difficult. Life, the whole Abigail thing, the…China thing. It just all seems so…out of my control. I hate that."

Brian looked at him with interest. "Is there a China thing?"

Campbell was a little surprised he'd said that aloud. But that was how Brian was. He made you forget to be cautious. "Is there for *you?*" Campbell asked. "You've spent time with her."

"No. I like her. She's lively and smart and I always have fun in her company. But I think of her as a sister, not a girlfriend."

Yeah, Campbell thought. If only his own reaction were that simple. She *wasn't* the sister he'd clashed with so much, she was just another young woman. But instead of clearing her away as a problem, that fact seemed to root her in place. They weren't blood-related, and now his mind insisted on creating these sexual fantasies about the two of them.

"I'm just discovering," Brian said, looking up at the stars, "that you have to relinquish the need to control. Control is what my father's all about and look where it's gotten him. He has a huge conglomerate worth megabucks, but he's all alone. I'm the bastard child, and yet I have all of you Abbotts. I've learned you have to relax about directing the way things go."

"You like being in business for yourself?"

"I do." Brian obviously meant what he said. "I don't have to worry about the Dow, NASDAQ, the S&P 500, or what Alan Greenspan predicts. I just have to give special care to the day to day running of Brian's General Store and Boat Rental. Keep the shelves stocked, the boats safe and running, and enjoy the people who come and go. On one level, I don't think I've ever been happier."

"But on another level?" Campbell asked.

Brian sighed and took another swallow of champagne. "On another level, I feel as though I'm on vacation, that I can't expect to be this happy forever. That I have to apply myself, get serious about my life, do something significant."

"Isn't that contrary to your let-things-happen-the-way-they're-supposed-to-happen theory?"

"Yeah, I guess. But it's a strong feeling, anyway—I tend to trust those. It's what led me to tell Cordie to tell Killian not to buy the Florida Shops."

Brian had saved the Abbotts from Girard's manipulations. His instincts were obviously sound.

"You remind me of me," Campbell said, taking a gulp of champagne, then leaning back on his elbow on the Lincoln's hood. "I'm always looking for the right direction. It'd be so much easier if fate just dropped a neon sign in front of your face."

Brian leaned forward, elbows on his knees, the glass held in his two hands as he studied the lacelike rills of surf in the darkness. "Yeah, but life's a journey. We're supposed to find the signs, pick our own roads."

"How did an old corporate man like you get so poetic about life?"

"When it's clear your father doesn't like you much less love you, and your mother always looks at you with sadness, as though you're responsible for her having lost something, you spend a lot of time wondering about things, thinking them through. Being poetic softens the edges of the harsh truths."

"Your father was a jerk."

"I know. But when you're a child, wanting to please a parent and earn his praise, you don't know that. All you know is that this person is supposed to love you, and he doesn't."

"Yeah." He'd heard Killian say the same thing about his natural mother, the woman who'd also given birth to Sawyer and Brian. He could only imagine how raising the child her husband had had with another woman had affected Girard's wife. "Your mother always seemed to adore you."

Brian looked back at him, his smile a little sad. "I think she did in a way. I loved her. But I imagine every time she looked at me, she saw glimpses of Susannah Abbott and couldn't help feeling betrayed. She never said that to me, never even hinted that I wasn't hers, but I used to see things in her eyes I didn't understand. She died still holding the secret from the world."

Campbell sat up again, feeling the need to support Brian somehow. "You've inherited a great house from your grandmother, and you have a small but dependable business. And you used to be an only child, but now you have three brothers. If we find Abby, you'll have a sister, too."

"Right. I value all of that. But the same applies to you and yet you're looking for something else. Who can explain what pushes and drives us?"

Campbell conceded that. "As the last two bachelors in the family, we're going to have to hang together on our right to be independent."

They toasted that and poured more champagne, which they drank in a pensive but comfortable silence.

"You should stay at the house tonight," Campbell said. "I picked you up, but I'm not sure I'm sober enough to take you home."

Brian nodded. "I'll stay in the boathouse."

"There's an empty room…."

"I like the boathouse."

It was filled with old furniture from when Chloe re-decorated the house, and was a quiet, comfortable retreat when the house was full or someone needed solitude. It was down a narrow lane directly behind the house.

They climbed back into the car and Campbell drove the short distance back to the house slowly, Brian holding the champagne and glasses. Campbell parked the limo, then took the bottle and glasses and said goodnight. The spotlights in the garden lit the path to the boathouse as Brian headed for it.

Campbell let himself in through the dark and quiet library. He put the bottle and glasses down on the granite counter, then fell onto the leather sofa with a groan.

He jumped a foot when a female voice right beside him said, "I seem to have come through the baby shower in better condition than you did your dinner party."

Chapter Five

China enjoyed Campbell's shocked response.

He gasped, a hand to his heart. "China! You just scared me out of my old age."

She elbowed him. "You probably wouldn't be able to decide where to spend it, anyway. You'll still be looking for where you want to be." That was a little snide, but the shower had been hard on her, what with all those young women, some of them pregnant, talking about homes and families and all the things that simply didn't exist for her right now. "I take it the party was a success?"

"Yes, thank you," he replied, relaxing against the back of the sofa. "Although Killian, Sawyer and Daniel were anxious to get back home. Would have completely ruined the spontaneity of the thing if Brian hadn't been along."

"What did you do?"

"We dropped them off, then drove to the end of the road to the beach and sat on the hood of the limo, drinking champagne."

She smiled in the shadows. "Such wild behavior."

He must have heard the smile in her voice. "Well," he replied a little defensively, "I wasn't looking for a wild time, exactly, just…" He hesitated, unsure of how to put it.

"I know," she said with a sigh. "Respite from the question."

He leaned away from her to turn on the lamp. A little puddle of light lit his furrowed brow and questioning gaze, leaving her in shadow. She hadn't meant to say those words. It was just that she thought she understood how he felt, and they came out of their own accord.

"What question?" he asked.

"The question we're both dealing with for very different reasons. Where we belong."

She expected him to be annoyed. He usually hated it when she got personal. But he seemed more focused on her than himself. "The family wants you to stay," he said.

"Yes. And they want you to stay, too, but it doesn't really answer the inner question, does it? Before either of us belongs anywhere, we're going to have to belong to ourselves. Be comfortable in our skin."

He arched a skeptical eyebrow. "Maybe you've overthought this a little."

She nodded. "That's what I do. Janet's always on me about it. Boyfriends run away in droves."

"Brian has this theory that we can't be happy until we give up control and let things happen the way they're supposed to happen."

"Really. So you were thinking while you were drinking champagne."

"I'm always thinking." He winced at her. "That doesn't mean you and I have that in common, too, does it?"

"Not to worry. You'll be gone soon."

"If Janet is Abby, then you're off to northern Canada to find your family?"

"Depends, I guess, on what she's discovered." China had already considered this in the dark of night. "Maybe…there isn't anybody."

"You know my family would welcome you here." His eyes were serious, and she was suddenly very aware of his arm along the back of the sofa. She tried not to think about the strong hands that had held her in comfort when she'd learned she wasn't an Abbott. Something tightened in her throat.

She sat forward. "I know. But I can't assume a life that doesn't belong to me. And if Janet is Abby, she'll need time to get acquainted with all of you, to learn where she fits." China thought that Campbell could really use a good dose of her hopeful, effervescent sister's positive outlook. "I hope if she is Abby that you'll take time to come back and get to know her. She's quite wonderful."

"I promise I will," he said gravely. He, too, sat forward. "You'll have to stay to help her settle in."

"That won't take long. She's open and funny and everyone loves her right away."

He looked into China's eyes and said with surprising sincerity, "I'll worry about you."

The simple statement took her breath away. She had to think before she spoke. "You know I'm very competent," she said with a voice that sounded a little thin. "I'll be fine."

She knew he heard her vulnerability. She hated that. She said a hasty good-night and stood to leave.

He stood with her and caught her wrist.

The simple gesture was both wonderful and awful, and she recognized it as a line that shouldn't be crossed. On this side was the sharp love-hate thing they'd had going since the moment they'd first met. On the other was something she was afraid to think about, feelings she didn't understand and shouldn't indulge, emotions that would further complicate the giant knot of their relationship.

"I need to know," he said softly, "that you're going to be all right." He drew her closer to him as he spoke, his hand on her elbow, then her shoulder, then the back of her waist.

She was going to choke. She had no air, or too much; she wasn't sure because she couldn't draw in air or expel it. The opportunity to be gone before that line was crossed was disappearing.

They'd left the pool of light and now were both in shadow. She could see the always-present gleam of his intensity in his eyes, the white of his teeth. The smell of the ocean still clung to him, and there was a dangerous air to the pulled-away tie, the open collar button of his shirt.

She put her hands on his arms in an effort to hold herself away, but she felt hard muscle there and remembered how surprised she'd been by the comfort to be found in these arms. The memory drew her closer as inexorably as his hands did now.

"Can't I just…promise?" she whispered.

His eyes were roving her face, devouring her feature by feature, lingering on her mouth, moving away, coming back.

"I'd need it verified somehow," he whispered back. "Sealed." And then he lowered his head to kiss her.

The line was not only crossed but obliterated. The man with whom she'd fought all those weeks now enfolded her in his embrace like a lover and opened his mouth over hers.

She should run, she thought. It was the only sensible reaction. This could never be.

But she was ensnared in the centrifugal power that was part of everything he did. She always thought it so unnecessary, so exhausting, yet at this point of personal uncertainty, she was happy to let it take her.

His lips were warm and bold, like the man himself. With a hand in her hair, he teased her lips with kisses and nibbles until she gasped, then he invaded her open mouth, looking for response.

Her response was right there ready to go, had been for weeks. All the undefined tension and unfocused emotion in their efforts to work together had collected on the surface of her consciousness and now exploded like Fourth of July fireworks.

Life had been so even before she'd come to Shepherd's Knoll, before she'd ever looked into Campbell Abbott's eyes. Now it was like roller-skating down a set of stairs, bumpy, death-defying, terrifying.

And yet she couldn't remember ever being as invested in life and its potential as she was at this moment.

She kissed him back, catching his intensity, feelings

she'd tried to pretend didn't exist erupting inside her. She was burning up, inside and out. Passion, she wondered in a detached part of her brain, or self-destruction?

He must have wondered, too, because he caught her arms suddenly and held her away. Drunk on him, she needed a moment to reestablish her balance.

When she could focus again, she had difficulty interpreting the dark emotion in his eyes. It looked remarkably like a sense of betrayal, but that wasn't logical. And the hands that continued to hold her arms were still tender, though she wouldn't have wanted to try to escape them.

Then she realized what he must be thinking, what he'd suspected from the day she arrived. That she'd come to find a way into the family in one way or another. This kiss had been a test to see if she'd be willing to use him.

She gasped at that discovery, then growled over it and struggled against him until he had to release her or hurt her.

"You're *such* an idiot!" she accused, and ran around him to the hallway as he watched her in frozen surprise. She raced up the stairs to her room.

After she closed her door, she checked her cell phone for messages on the chance she'd missed a call from Janet. But she hadn't. She tore off her clothes, furious with herself for crossing the line—or letting Campbell drag her across it—then curled into the middle of her bed and socked her pillow. She wished she could sob into it for some release of this giant, barbed emotion, but she was too angry for that.

Fortunately that degree of anger was exhausting and she finally felt herself drift off, hoping to dream of running over Campbell with the tractor.

CAMPBELL CAME IN from the orchard to find the house in turmoil. He'd gotten up early, hurried out to the vintage orchard and the ongoing job of thinning the crop. He hadn't slept a wink and knew it showed in his face. There'd be questions, concerns, and he didn't want to deal with them.

When he walked into the kitchen two hours later, hoping for a cup of coffee, he found Kezia on the phone, sounding desperate. "Yes, Doctor. No, she's conscious, but she's having difficulty breathing and she seems to be in pain. Yes, I know, but she won't let us call an ambulance, gets even more agitated when we try to do it. Please, Dr. Doyle, come to the house. Yes, I know all that, too, but she won't be budged. Please."

Campbell heard the second half of that conversation on his way up the stairs, taking them two at a time.

At first he'd been afraid Cordie's pregnancy had been in danger, but the description of the woman who refused to get into an ambulance fit his mother to perfection. He remembered an incident years ago when she'd fallen in the garden. She had clearly broken her foot but refused to let anyone call an ambulance. His father had already passed away, Killian and Sawyer had been away from the house, and he'd tried to overrule her to no avail. She'd made such a fuss that Kezia had sided with her, and Campbell had finally driven her to the hospital in his old Camaro.

"You won't be able to get in the back with a broken foot," he'd reasoned calmly, "and there won't be room for you to stretch out in the front."

She'd made do with the front seat and several pillows stacked under her leg so that her foot didn't touch the floor.

He could feel all that old exasperation rising in him now as he reached the top of the stairs and ran down the hall to his mother's room.

She was sitting up in bed, pillows propped behind her, Tante Bijou at the foot of the bed in her wheelchair giving orders in French as everyone else in the household gathered around. Chloe drew in air in difficult gasps.

Sophie, who'd apparently been called, sat on the edge of the bed in jeans and a sweatshirt, taking her pulse.

"Where are…the children?" his mother asked with difficulty.

"Shh," Sophie scolded, then after waiting a few seconds released her hand and placed it beside her. "They're with the neighbors," she said. "Your pulse is a little elevated, Chloe, but not very much. What were you doing when this happened?"

"Just…sitting here," she said, dropping a hand on an open notebook that lay beside her, "making redecorating plans. Thinking about…about Abby coming home." She picked Campbell out of the crowd. "About Campbell leaving, China wanting to leave."

China moved the notebook to sit beside her. "I'm not going *tomorrow*," she teased gently, taking her hand. "I'll wait until Janet gets here, until the tests are taken and the results come back."

"I want my family together," Chloe said in a strained voice. "I've waited so long."

Campbell pushed his way between Killian and Sawyer. "Call the ambulance," he said, worried about her uncharacteristic agitation, "and we'll put her in it."

"She doesn't want—" China began with an icy glance at him. Last night, after that mind-bending kiss, her expression had become hot and angry. He had no idea what was going on in her mind and didn't even want to guess.

"I think we should do what's best for her," he interrupted, "not what she wants. She's clearly not thinking straight."

"You always do what *you* want," she challenged.

"My life isn't at risk!" he retorted. "Mom, you're going to the hospital." He reached for the phone on her bedside table.

"Her doctor's on the way." Kezia appeared in the doorway. "He says he'll be here in five minutes."

Campbell replaced the phone.

Sophie shooed everyone toward the door. "Let's let her relax a little." She put an arm around Campbell's shoulders and said quietly, "That's good advice for you, too. She's in no imminent danger, I promise you."

He stopped in the doorway to frown at her in affectionate annoyance. "You're not going to start telling me what to do, too, are you?"

She smiled back at him. "I have three children. It's a habit."

With China standing behind him, waiting to leave the room, he bit back a response and walked out into the hallway. China followed, closing the door behind her.

"I was concerned for Mom's safety," he said as she walked with him to the stairs. "Not insensitive to what she wanted."

"Sophie doesn't think she's in danger," she countered, "so I don't see why your mother couldn't be indulged a little. This has been a difficult time for her."

"It has. But if she's having some kind of heart episode, even doctors can't predict what will happen next. I'd hate to have her stubborn refusal to ride in an ambulance mean she wouldn't live to see Abby, after all. Or that Abby would lose her just days before she's about to find her."

China stopped, indignation so ripe in her she bristled. But he could see in her eyes that she hadn't considered that point, and admitting it was going to cost her.

He walked on, not particularly interested in making her pay the price.

She caught the crook of his arm and yanked him to a stop. Her touch was so new to him, such a unique experience, that he allowed it to prolong the moment.

"You're right," she said defensively.

A little surprised by that admission, he resisted the impulse to lean into her, the same impulse he should not have listened to the night before. "Even idiots are occasionally right," he replied, and moved on again.

"Right about *her*," she called after him, keeping her voice down in deference to his mother beyond the door. "Wrong about *me*."

He'd reached the end of the corridor before he realized he didn't know what the second half of that declaration meant. He stopped and turned. She remained in the middle of the hallway.

"What do you mean?" he asked plainly.

She looked heavenward in supplication. "Please. That kiss was…" She hesitated a moment, then apparently unwilling or unable to say just what it was, skipped on. "Then you pushed me away like I was going to give you beri-beri or something."

He recalled that moment. The kiss had been…he couldn't come up with the right word for it, either. But it had made him feel like a character in a snow globe. He'd felt one way about things, and now…he wasn't so sure. Everything in his world was turned upside down, and cold stuff was falling all over him.

Impressed that she'd admitted the kiss had been significant to her—at least that was what he thought she'd meant—he had to be honest with her. To a point, anyway.

"I wasn't afraid of catching whatever it is you've got, if that's what you mean."

She came toward him, puzzled and apparently offended. "What I've *got?*"

"Whatever it is that makes you testy and argumentative," he replied.

She gasped. "*You* make me testy and argumentative!" Her voice squeaked with the effort to keep it down. "You tested me with that kiss of yours. You think I'm after the Abbott money!"

It took him a moment to assimilate that accusation. He couldn't remember anything that had ever passed between them that would make her think that.

"No, I don't," he said.

She made a scornful sound and walked around

him, headed for the stairs. He pulled her back into the relative privacy of the hallway. "Where did you get that idea?"

"You made it clear! First you kissed me like some hero heading off on a fatal mission, then when I responded, you withdrew. What else could it mean? You wanted to see if I'd tumble to your charms, and when I did, it proved what you've suspected since the moment I arrived. That I'm after Abbott money. And since the DNA test proved I'm not Abby, you're thinking I'll find another way to claim the Abbott name. You."

"What?" he demanded. "That's insane. You're insane!"

"Go ahead and deny it."

"I do deny it! Emphatically and categorically."

She folded her arms. "Then why did you push me away and look at me as though I'd somehow betrayed you?"

He opened his mouth to insist that he hadn't done that, then realized he may very well have. Kissing her had been an impulse that had turned into something more significant than he'd intended. He remembered thinking in his momentary confusion that he hadn't meant it to be that important, hadn't wanted it to be. So the fact that it was had to be her fault.

He couldn't tell her that he'd had to back away from that kiss and all it could mean because he was afraid of its potential at a time when he finally had a chance to get away from the family and Shepherd's Knoll.

"Because I didn't want you to think it was more than it was," he said. That was disgustingly egotistical and a bald-faced lie, but it was the best of two bad choices.

She blew air out from between her lips in scorn.

"You really think you're that attractive to me that I'll fall apart if you don't kiss me again?"

"You were as into it as I was."

"Maybe I was just being polite and careful of your feelings. You're a little fragile since you've decided to leave."

He was sure that was intended to annoy him and cut him down to size. He was annoyed. "You're never polite to me or careful of my feelings" he argued. "You were into it."

"You flatter yourself."

"Okay." He squared off with her. "Let's do it again and see whose memory can be trusted."

Panic flared in her eyes. He knew it!

"That won't prove anything. Being prepared, I can withhold emotion if I want to, or I can pretend it. Either way, how would you know if your point was made? Or mine?"

"I'd know," he insisted. But realizing there might be something in her argument, he conceded. "Okay, then. We'll wait until you're not expecting it. Until I can take you by surprise."

"I'm always prepared for anything," she said with a cool smile and superior lift of her eyebrow. "And you're leaving. You'll just have to believe me, Campbell."

He would have disputed that the truth was in her eyes, but there were footsteps on the stairs and the doctor appeared with Cordie at his side. China took that opportunity to flee, and Campbell went down to the kitchen, desperately in need of coffee.

Within an hour everyone but Sophie had gathered

around the kitchen table while Killian handed the doctor a steaming mug. "I've encouraged her to try to get some sleep," the doctor said, smiling around the room. "Your mother is fine. I think she suffered an anxiety attack. She told me she was up most of the night creating this plan to renovate the house."

Everyone looked at everyone else in surprise.

"She showed me sketches," he went on, "of rooms on the third floor renovated for Sawyer and his family, a nursery for the new babies, and a couple of other changes she wants to make."

Everyone continued to gape.

"She's never mentioned this," Killian said. "I didn't even suspect it was on her mind."

The doctor smiled kindly. "She probably needed something positive to claim her focus. You have to remember that though she's chic and youthful, she's growing older, and while all of you have important things to do, they take you away from her. Mothers are supposed to be prepared for that, but you have the unusual circumstance of your missing sister. She's managed to suppress her grief and what has to be daily pain, so that she could help all of you get on with your lives. But every moment of her life, she's had to cope with the fact that her baby's missing."

Killian turned to Sawyer. "Maybe I'll have to send Lew Weston to London."

Weston was Killian's resident genius and general troubleshooter.

Sophie walked into the room. "Chloe's finally asleep," she announced. "Tante Bijou is watching her."

"Good." The doctor nodded his approval, then shook his head at Killian's suggestion. "Your mother doesn't want any of you to change your plans. But I think it might be a good idea if she went somewhere, had a change of scene. She explained that you're expecting word any day from a young woman who might be your sister. I know that's a lot of her tension. Rather than letting her wait around, I think you should send her somewhere with Tante Bijou." The doctor said their aunt's name with beautiful French enunciation. He'd treated her a time or two in the past. "She can be back quickly if there's news of your sister. I understand, in fact, that that's the plan for all of you."

They nodded collectively.

"Good. Then let's let life continue and find your mother something else to think about for a week or so."

"Sawyer and I and my children are going to Vermont to meet my family," Sophie said. "What if we took her and Tante Bijou with us? We're driving rather than flying, so the trip won't be too difficult for them."

The doctor nodded with enthusiasm. "I think that's perfect. New people, new sights. And close enough that you can come right back with a few hours' notice."

Sawyer put an arm around Sophie and kissed the top of her head.

While the doctor fielded a few more questions, Campbell slipped out of the kitchen and into his office, quietly pushing the door closed.

He lifted a limp Versace off his chair and sat down, the cat curling up again on his lap. He called Flamingo Gables, staring at the stack of packed boxes while waiting for someone to pick up. When he finally reached his new employer, he told him he had to delay his arrival.

There was a moment of surprised silence. Campbell took advantage of it to explain that his mother had taken ill and they were waiting to hear from a young woman who might be Abigail.

"Thornton's leaving Monday," the man said in a tone that was worried, though still sympathetic. Thornton was the manager Campbell was supposed to replace.

"I know," Campbell replied. "And I'm so sorry. But I have no control over this. My family's in turmoil and I can't, in all conscience, leave right now. The only reassurance I can give you is that when I do get there, I'll apply the same sense of responsibility to my work for you. But if you have to replace me in the meantime, I understand."

There was a groan, then a sigh. "We'll make do as long as we can, but that may happen if you delay too long."

"I understand."

Another sigh. "All right. Keep in touch."

"I will." Campbell hung up the phone, not happy but surprisingly unburdened by the decision he'd made. The freedom to learn what he was capable of had to take second place to easing his mother's mind.

He'd known she wanted him to stay at Shepherd's Knoll, but he'd felt it was a simple case of maternal concern for a youngest son. And Killian and Sawyer were so tied to home now that they had families, he was sure they'd be here for her.

He hadn't given serious thought to how much of her own pain she'd suppressed to make certain the lives of her children moved on. They had all suffered when Abby was taken, but they had the busy job of growing up to do, and their father had the company. Their mother, though, had stayed home to be available to all of them, and she doubtless thought about her missing daughter every time one of them had a birthday or reached some other milestone.

Then China had appeared and hope had been dangled in front of his mother, then withdrawn when China proved not to be Abigail. Would the same thing happen with China's sister, Janet? He hoped not.

He imagined that the renovation plans the doctor talked about were a place to focus her energy, something else to think about so that the possibilities didn't make her insane.

He'd see what he could do about them while she was gone. And he was sure she'd be happier knowing that a family member was home on the chance that Janet appeared.

All right. Contrarily, even though his immediate plans had disintegrated, he felt as though he'd taken charge of his life.

He left his office by the outside door and strode toward the garage, intent on going to town for printer paper. The chore could have waited, but he had a sudden burst of nervous energy and had to drive somewhere. He considered it fortunate that China, in a brimmed straw hat, with a straw hobo bag over her shoulder, was headed in the same direction.

Something else in his life he had to take charge of.

Chapter Six

China pulled her purse off her shoulder as she walked and dug inside for her keys. Kezia was sending her to town for a bottle of Riesling for Chloe's favorite dish, Coq au Riesling.

She felt sorry that her search for her family had heaped yet more grief on the woman who'd so wanted to be her mother. She could only hope that this whole experience would have a happy ending for the Abbotts, after all.

One day she would find her own fairy-tale ending. She would—

Her thoughts were halted abruptly when her purse caught on something and stopped her in her tracks. She slipped it off her shoulder as she turned, wondering what on earth—

That was another thought halted abruptly when she found herself looking into Campbell's purposeful eyes. He had the other end of her purse strap. Oh, no. The threatened kiss. Well, it might surprise him to know that all she needed to prepare herself for the assault of his…

She was going to have to give up thinking. She

watched him drop her purse to the ground, pull her to him, reach for the brim of her hat and toss it after her purse. One hand cupped the back of her head, the other her bottom as he set out to prove his theory that…that…

She couldn't remember what it had been. What hers had been. Why they'd even argued over it.

And she'd been wrong about the assault. His embrace was the perfect combination of tenderness and confidence, his touch at once reverent and possessive. There wouldn't have been enough time in eternity to prepare to defend herself against it. And the insidious thing was that he made her feel she belonged right there in his arms.

He kissed her boldly, deeply, and when she had to gasp for air, he kissed the line of her jaw to her ear, then down the cord of her neck to her shoulder, bared by the tank top.

She was too witless to kiss him back, though she felt herself leaning into him, unconsciously begging him not to stop. Her brain was empty, her sense of touch apparently the only thing at work in her body. And it worked overtime as his hands wandered all over her.

It was as though the surface of her skin had ignited, and every nerve ending beneath fluttered. It felt almost like an illness as her brain struggled to function.

She had terminal hots for Campbell Abbott.

A red whorl was beginning to form behind her eyes when he finally let her go. She reached out to steady herself and he held on to her until she did.

The moment she dropped her hands from him, he snatched up her things. He put the purse on her shoulder, the hat on her head, then leaned down to kiss her chastely on the mouth.

"Good thing you didn't put money on it," he said, chucking her under the chin. "Need a lift to town?"

Euphoria was slowly being replaced by respect for his incomparable skill—and deep concern about what her response to it meant. Not to mention irritation at his obvious self-satisfaction.

Not that he wasn't entitled to it.

Thank God, he was leaving soon.

"I'll drive myself, thank you," she replied with commendable calm.

"Okay. See you at dinner." He strode into the garage with all the confidence of a man who'd effectively made his point.

EVERYONE GATHERED around the dinner table. Because of the events of the morning, the menu had been changed from Campbell's favorite meal to Chloe's.

Seated at the head of the table in a teal silk mandarin-style dressing gown, Chloe still looked a little pale. She studied the chicken baked with wine and onions and mushrooms, and addressed Kezia as she placed a platter of green beans almandine in the middle of the table, "I asked you to prepare a pork roast for Campbell."

Kezia smiled. "Yes, Mrs. Abbott. But the reason for the party has changed."

Chloe looked disgruntled. "I am much better and feel very silly to have upset everyone like that. I wanted this to be very special for Campbell." He was seated at her left, and she reached a hand out to catch his.

"There's no longer need for a farewell party," Killian announced from her right. "He's decided to stay for a while."

Chloe exclaimed in French and reached over to hug Campbell. A cheer rose around the table. China smiled when Winfield smiled at her, but inside she was thinking, *Aaaggghhh!* The day after tomorrow, everyone but the staff at Shepherd's Knoll was taking off in different directions, except China, who'd promised to wait for word of Janet, and…now…Campbell.

Her head began to ache.

"China and I will get the renovation moving while you're gone," Campbell promised.

China smiled dutifully when everyone turned to her. "I don't know anything about renovating or decorating," she said, hoping it would get her out of working with him.

"I have a friend whose sister works for a decorating firm in Boston. She's home for the summer. We can show her Mom's sketches and she can get us going."

"Who is your friend, *ma chère*?" Chloe asked.

"Billy Sandusky's sister, Karen."

"Billy Sandusky with the helicopter?" Killian asked. "The one who flew you home from your Flamingo Gables interview?"

Campbell nodded. "Yeah. The lawyer."

Sawyer looked up from helping Emma serve herself. "Billy Sandusky is a lawyer? What's she doing with a helicopter?"

"She flew one in Desert Storm. She likes it. It gets her to the city or wherever she has to go in a fraction of the time."

Chloe shook her head in amazement. "The people you know," she said. "And this Karen. Does she drive a spaceship or anything?"

There was laughter around the table. "No. She's quite the lady. You'll like her. You explain to me what the sketches mean and what you have in mind and I'll pass it on."

"Why do I have to be involved?" China asked.

"To interpret all the things I don't understand," he said. "You know, fabric names, cornices, that sort of stuff."

Now was probably not the time to tell him she didn't know what a cornice was, either.

Cordie explained it to him, though, while Sawyer passed China the bowl of roasted red potatoes. "I'm glad you're staying," he said softly, holding the bowl for her so that she could serve herself. "He likes to think of himself as a misfit here, as the odd man out. Killian and I have given up trying to make him see the light, but maybe you'll have some luck."

China made a face. "What makes you think I have any influence over him?"

Sawyer grinned. "I saw the kiss."

She stifled a sound of distress and lowered her voice even further. "He was just trying to make a point."

"Did he?"

She sighed and admitted grudgingly, "Yes."

"See? Kisses like that are chemistry. And the two of you have had it from the instant you met. I think you hated each other because the attraction was there and you thought it shouldn't be because you might be brother and sister. But you're not, so it can. Enough potatoes. Can you really eat six of them?"

China looked down at the potatoes she'd collected on her plate in her agitation and replaced five of them. "Thank you," she said, ignoring the interested looks around the table.

"How long are you staying in Vermont?" China asked as Sawyer passed on the bowl.

"Just a week. Think you can manage to coexist with Campbell that long?"

"Winfield will be here to prevent me from killing him."

"You might not realize it, but it's a big step that Campbell's agreed to stay. Underneath that gruff exterior, he's really very lovable."

"Uh-huh," she said with complete lack of conviction.

China helped Kezia clear after the huge dinner so that everyone else could finishing packing. Daniel was driving Killian and Cordie to the airport first thing in the morning, and Sawyer arranged to rent a van so that he would have room for his two new passengers and Tante Bijou's wheelchair.

"You're sure Tante Bijou doesn't mind the drive?" China asked Chloe when she was called to her room. "If she'd prefer to stay home, I wouldn't mind looking after her."

Chloe tucked silky underthings into an inside pocket of her suitcase. "She loves to travel. And now that she is feeling so much better, she's excited to see something new."

On her way back to her dresser, Chloe pushed China into a slipper chair and handed her a brocade-covered notebook. "This is what I was thinking we should do to make sure everyone can be comfortable here."

China looked through the book, surprised to find detailed sketches of the turret room, the third floor, the sunporch, and suggestions for an addition onto the back. She'd cut pages out of magazines, stuck in fabric swatches, wallpaper samples and paint chips.

"You've given this a lot of thought," China said, turning the book at a right angle to study a clipping of a masculine bedroom done in plaids.

"I started thinking about it when Killian told me he and Cordie were getting back together. I was taking care of Tante Bijou at the time, and when I sat with her, I looked through magazines and cut out things I thought would work for us. Then as things began to happen—Sawyer and Sophie and the children, the addition of Brian to our family—the project began to grow."

"You want me?" Campbell appeared in the doorway in the dark cotton slacks and sweater he'd worn at dinner. His dark good looks and preference for dark colors always made him look as though the Jolly Roger should be flying over his head.

Yes, China thought silently, though she knew he was speaking to his mother. *I think I do.*

"Yes, *petit chou.* Come and look at my book with China and tell me if you like my ideas. Can your friend make them work, do you think?"

Campbell took the book from China and sat with it on the window seat. He flipped pages, looked through all the things she'd tucked in. "I'm sure she can make it work," he said, "but *you'll* want to talk with her. What if we just get her to walk through, maybe add her own ideas, give us some estimates, so that when you come home you'll know what's involved, time- and money-wise. This looks like a whole new wing."

"Yes. I was thinking we should add a room for Brian over a sunporch on the south side. Then we'll want the third floor to be child-friendly for Sophie and Sawyer's children. But I'm afraid it won't be finished until long after the wedding."

Campbell agreed with a single nod. "But they'll have a home of their own, Mom."

"I know, but when they're here, I want them to be comfortable. And for parties and holidays they might want to stay with us, even though they're nearby. The same with Brian. He has that wonderful Gothic monstrosity of his grandmother's, but when it's family time, it would be nice if he had his own space here."

He flipped back several pages. "I like the sunporch. It's huge."

"Yes. I'm imagining long summer evenings there."

Campbell got an image of that, the sweet-salty fragrance of the night, the taste of Kezia's peach martinis, China beside him on the glider. It occurred to him that it was strange he was thinking in terms of family evenings on the sunporch when he'd been so anxious to get away. But his mother's anxiety spell had changed his plans and temporarily altered his reality, so he was free to imagine whatever he wanted.

But…China? He looked up from the book and into her eyes. She looked as intrigued yet perplexed as he was.

He handed her the book and stood. "When you're

packed," he told his mother, "I'll carry your bags down-stairs so all you'll have to do in the morning is have breakfast and take off. Are those Tante Bijou's bags in the hall?"

"Yes. Now, you're not going to badger China while I'm gone?"

"*Maman*," he replied, "she's the one who tends to badger me. You might speak to her."

Chloe ran a pointing finger from one to the other. "You will not badger each other, but be supportive," she decreed firmly. "Is that clear?"

"Yes, ma'am," China said.

Chloe turned to Campbell.

He crossed his fingers behind his back in the old childhood gesture that nullified the promise. "Yes, *Maman*." When Chloe turned her back to add a bag of toiletries to her suitcase, he held up the crossed fingers in China's face.

She slapped them away.

His mother turned back quickly, looking suspicious-ly from one to the other. "It would be nice," she said, "if some thoughtful child brought me a cup of tea."

"That would be me," China said, standing. "That is, I'm the thoughtful one, though I'm not your child."

Chloe hugged her. "You will always be my child. But I think it will take both of you to make the tea. Now, go. Before I expire of thirst."

China sailed out of the room ahead of Campbell. He made a face at his mother for her manipulations, and as he followed China from the room, she swatted him with a pink slipper.

China put the kettle on to boil and he reached into a cupboard for his mother's favorite fat mug. On it were painted the words *C'est Toujours la Fête*. It's always a party.

Campbell put the mug on the counter in front of China and she dropped a tea bag into it. "What I don't understand," she whispered as though no time had elapsed between now and their most recent argument, "is if you didn't want me to think that that first kiss was more than it was, why was it so important to prove my vulnerability to you with a second kiss? It doesn't make sense."

"You never make sense," he replied. "Seemed like the perfect way to communicate with you."

"Campbell…"

"Okay." He leaned against the counter, his hands braced on the rim. "It was your claim that you were just being polite by responding to me the first time I kissed you, when it was clear that wasn't true. You responded because it touched you, just as it touched me."

She didn't seem to know how to answer. "Well…what's the point in admitting we were affected," she asked finally, "when it wouldn't be smart to do anything about it? You're going to leave eventually and so am I."

"Because lies are a disturbance in the order of things."

"Thank you, Obe Wan. But it's not a lie, it's just a… a choice to let what could amount to a troublesome truth pass unnoticed."

"I noticed it," he said. "And so did you."

She reached for a pink bakery box on the counter and drew it toward her. It contained the star-shaped apricot tarts his mother loved so much.

"You think she'll want one of these with her tea?" she asked, getting a plate.

The innocent question was intended to distract him, he was sure. "No," he said patiently. "Not while she's packing."

China snatched one from the box, ripped off the point of a star with her teeth and retrieved another cup from the cupboard. "Well, I want one. You?"

"No, thank you."

The kettle boiled and filled the kitchen with its shrill whistle. China sat on a stool, ignoring it. "You get that," she said. "You're the good child who decided to stay so your mother wouldn't be upset. You take her the tea. I'll just sit here and drown my sorrows in pastry."

The room fell suddenly quiet as he lifted the kettle off the burner and poured hot water over the tea bag. "What sorrows? You mean because you're developing a thing for me?"

"I'm not developing it. Yes, it's there, but I'm not developing it."

"So I have to nurture our relationship all by myself?" He let the tea get a nice deep brown, then removed the bag and put the mug on a saucer. He took down a second cup, brewed tea in it and handed it to her.

She popped the last bite of tart into her mouth and accepted the mug with a nod. "Thank you. You can't do that. Love—" She stopped, clearly wishing she hadn't used that word. "Attraction," she corrected, "takes two. And I'm not participating."

HE SMILED, his virile charm in place despite the mug and saucer he held. "That's probably smart, actually. What you shouldn't do right now is split your focus."

"What do you mean?" She dunked the tea bag distractedly. He was up to something.

He shrugged, moving toward the door. "You and me together might be too big for you. You still have the family-search thing to do, and I, at least, know where I'm going next."

"I thought you were trying to find yourself, too."

"I know who I am, I'm just looking for my place. You, on the other hand, seem to think who you are depends on where you sprang from."

She slipped off the stool, curiously annoyed by that assessment of her situation. "You make me sound selfish."

He denied that with a frown. "No, just confused."

"But…say there was something going on between us. Wouldn't *you* want to know who my family is?"

"No. Well, I mean if they were around, I'd like to know them, but if you didn't know who they were, I wouldn't care."

"You say that now."

"I'd say that anytime. The only hitch would be that *you'd* care. Excuse me. I'd better take this up before it gets cold."

He left the kitchen and China finished her tea, staring moodily out the kitchen window. Just her luck that she'd come to Shepherd's Knoll hoping to find some answers about herself, but had succeeded only in turning up more questions.

Life was moving in the wrong direction. She had to do something about that. And she had a sneaking suspicion that admitting feelings for Campbell would hinder rather than help the situation.

EVERYONE WAS UP EARLY the next morning to wave off Killian and Cordie. After Daniel drove away, Sawyer pulled the rented van up to the front of the house, and Campbell and Winfield helped load a wide assortment of suitcases and totes. Emma held a new Barbie case possessively while Eddie showed off his Game Boy. Gracie had a small stack of teen and fashion magazines. The children were obviously excited about the trip.

Campbell teased Sawyer about buying the children's affections. "Darn right," Sawyer admitted. "Keeping them happy and hopefully quiet should help all of us."

He settled the children comfortably in the back, Winfield lifted Tante Bijou into the middle seat, and Chloe climbed in after her. A bag with treats for the drive was stuffed in between the two bucket seats in the front, a thermos stashed in a drawer under the passenger seat.

Finally everyone was in the van, and China stood with Campbell, Winfield and Kezia to wave goodbye.

"Remember," Chloe cautioned as Winfield prepared to close the sliding door. She pointed at Campbell and China. "No fighting."

"Yeah, yeah," Campbell said, waving. China blew her a kiss without promising anything.

Winfield closed the door and Sawyer turned the key in the ignition. The children waved madly as the van pulled away.

China could already feel the tension building as the van reached the road to the highway, then made the turn and disappeared behind a row of vine maples.

A strange quiet fell over the landscape, usually such

a loud and vibrant place. Kezia and Winfield turned back to the house to resume their duties. Campbell bumped China with his elbow.

"Relax," he advised. "It's going to be all right. I promise not to surprise you with kisses unless you want me to."

"I don't," she assured him pleasantly. "And we should be focused on your mother's project, anyway. I was out on the south side early this morning, trying to imagine the addition. I think it'll be wonderful."

"Really?" He glanced at his watch. "It's just after eight now. How early were you up?"

"Sometime before six."

"Couldn't sleep?"

There was a subtle suggestion in the question that he'd been responsible.

"I was…restless," she replied offhandedly. "No big deal. Happens to me all the time."

"Nervous energy?" he asked.

"I went to bed early," she answered.

"I heard you moving around after midnight."

She rolled her eyes and turned toward the house, but stopped in exasperation before starting up the steps. "It wasn't the kiss, okay? And I'm a big girl, anyway. You think I've never been kissed before? That I haven't had relationships that have kept me up nights?"

He seemed to consider that a moment, looking into her eyes for help in reaching a conclusion. "Yes, to the 'been kissed before' question, but no to having relationships that kept you up nights."

He was absolutely right. She hated that. "And you come to that conclusion how?" she asked testily.

His eyes went to her lips with an intensity that brought back just how powerful his kisses had been. After a moment, he lifted his gaze to her eyes again, his own with a surprisingly serious expression, considering the teasing nature of this whole conversation.

"Because they had the surprise and wonder of discovery," he said finally. "I'll wager that's never kept you up nights before, but it did last night. It did me, too."

"I thought you agreed that I shouldn't split my focus," she reminded him in annoyance. "Yet here we are again, talking about us."

"Yeah. I think it's one of those things that's going to keep getting in our way until we deal with it."

"Then *you* deal with it. I'm going to pretend it isn't happening." She started up the steps, but he caught her arm, then bracketed her waist and lifted her down to his level again.

"Wha…?" she began, but he was already kissing her. It wasn't quite as intense as the last time, in fact, had a bite of humor in it, though the element of possession it contained was up a little from last time.

Good Lord, she thought in a part of her brain that was allowing her to analyze. *I sound like a weather report. Elements of this, percentages of that.*

She wedged a space between them and pushed him away. "What are you *doing?*" she demanded.

He smiled. "That's my way of dealing with it."

Chapter Seven

Karen Benning, Billy Sandusky's sister, arrived in the middle of the morning in a gleaming taupe SUV. A slender, leggy blonde—twice divorced, according to Kezia—she wore daffodil cotton slacks, a white V-necked sweater, yellow canvas slides on her feet and brilliant diamond studs at her ears. Her blue eyes were as bright as the studs, and her red, collagen-plumped lips glossy. She was, frankly, drop-dead gorgeous.

China, in from the orchard, tried desperately not to betray her envy while Campbell introduced her to Karen. He, too, had come in from the orchard, but sweat and dishevelment, while not very attractive on a woman, were sexy and curiously appealing on a man.

Karen looped her arm in his and suggested that he and China lead her through the areas his mother wanted her to work on. To Karen's credit, she did not dismiss China and devote all her attention to Campbell. She directed her suggestions to her as much as she did to him, and seemed genuinely friendly. She was just one of those women, China thought, her envy increasing, who possessed a naturally charming, unaffected style along with great looks. Though China remained flawlessly polite, she couldn't wait for the tour to be over. She felt gawky and tongue-tied and completely overshadowed.

And it didn't help that Karen looked respectfully through Chloe's book, praised her for her ideas and said that they could all be worked into a comfortable plan.

"Would you mind if I took the book," she asked Campbell, "and made some sketches for you to show your mother when she gets back?"

"Of course not." Her easy charm seemed to have polished his, leaving China feeling even clunkier. "She'll appreciate your interest. She put a lot of effort into it."

"I'll take good care of it." Karen offered him her hand, then reached for China's, and promised to be back with figures and a timetable before Chloe came home. She opened the SUV's door, took a pair of tiny-lensed sunglasses from the visor, then climbed in behind the wheel. She pulled away smoothly and quietly.

Campbell gazed after the departing car, one shoulder leaning against a front-porch pillar. "It's too bad I'm not into blondes," he said with a mournful shake of his head.

China didn't believe hair color would stop a man from being interested in a woman like Karen. "Oh, come on," she chided. "Certainly you're interested in a beautiful face, a shapely derriere, and charm that goes on as long as her legs."

He seemed surprised by China's generous description. "I thought all beautiful women hated other beautiful women."

"I wanted to," she admitted with a sigh, deciding to

ignore his backhanded compliment, "but, what's not to like? She's lovely looking, and nice to boot." She frowned at him in puzzlement. "How can you dismiss all that because her hair's the wrong color?"

He grinned. "Because I have all that in a brunette."

She folded her arms, refusing to acknowledge that she knew he meant her. "It's said that *gentlemen* prefer blondes."

"Okay, then I suppose that proves your point that I'm no gentleman."

She'd have liked to confirm that, but for all his contentious behavior and his surprise kisses, he'd been kind. When she'd learned she was an Abbott after all, he'd offered comfort and encouraged her to stay.

"I think it proves you should think seriously about getting glasses." She needed desperately to escape for a little while, to do something from her old life that would remind her that somewhere back there she'd started all this from a point of sanity. "If you'll excuse me for a little while, I'm going to town."

"I'll drive you," he offered. "I have to pick up a couple of things Daniel ordered from the auto-parts shop. I just need twenty minutes to shower and change. Meet you in the kitchen."

Had she wanted to voice objections to the plan, he wouldn't have heard them. He loped inside and was out of sight by the time she reached the foyer.

When she arrived in the kitchen, showered and changed into a white cotton sundress, he was waiting for her.

CAMPBELL LOVED HER in that dress. It was formfitting and youthful and showed off the tan she'd acquired working in the orchard in a tank top and shorts. She'd swept her mass of dark hair into a knot at the back of her head, curly ends spilling out of it and bouncing as she walked. Sunlight coming in from outside shone in it, burnishing the rich color and dancing as she moved her head.

And she wondered why he didn't prefer blondes.

He saw her look him over. He'd put on a pair of beige cotton slacks he seldom wore and a silky, short-sleeved white shirt his mother had bought for him in Paris. He wore dark loafers, instead of the boots he always wore in the orchard, and had even slapped on a little aftershave.

She seemed to appreciate his efforts, though he felt fairly certain she'd promised herself never to admit aloud that she liked anything about him.

He opened the kitchen door and gestured her through.

"Want me to drop you somewhere?" he asked when they were under way in his car. "Then we can meet up for lunch afterward."

"Yes. I was just going to do some shopping."

"For what?"

"Clothes. Shoes. Some personal things."

"Good. Merrick's is really the only place in town for women's clothes—it's good stuff, I'm told. And Clifford's Emporium has everything imaginable. Maybe you'll find the other things there."

"Okay. We should have asked Kezia if she needed anything."

"I did, but she said no."

"How thoughtful."

He slanted her a glance, wondering if she was being sarcastic, but she didn't seem to be. She was smiling, her face turned into the wind from the open window. The day was warm and sharply clear, sunlight glinting off the water and every window and piece of chrome.

"I have many good qualities," he said with feigned modesty, "but Killian and Sawyer have sainthood and heroism sewn up. I'm just looking for work I can be proud of and a life I can enjoy."

"So I bring out the cranky autocrat?" she teased.

He smiled at the road. "He appears in response to the smart-mouthed brat. Thank you for your exemplary behavior this morning, by the way."

"I'm just trying to lull you into a sense of security."

"That never happens to me. It's why I hired Winfield."

She seemed suddenly interested in why he had. "Has there ever been a threat against your family?" Then she shook her head. "Stupid question. Of course there was the kidnapping, but…apart from that."

"No. But it pays to be careful and to have hired muscle. I wanted to make sure whatever precautions we could put in place were taken."

"Sounds wise to me."

"Thank you. Mom gives me a lot of flack about it."

They'd reached downtown Losthampton and the quaint historic shopping area filled with upscale boutiques. He pulled into a parking space and China reached for the door handle. "Where do you want me to meet you and what time?"

"Hold on," he said. "I'll help you out."

"I can…"

He ignored her, walking around the car to open her door.

"I thought you weren't a gentleman." She accepted his hand and stepped out of the car with a taunting grin.

"I never said that. You just misinterpreted my preference for brunettes over blondes." He looked at her hair, glossy in the sunlight, and added, "And if you could see your hair, you'd never wonder why."

She put a fluttering hand to her hair, and looked a little embarrassed. "Thank you. Hair clips are one of the things I'm shopping for. I've lost a couple of them in the orchard. What time…?"

He caught her arm and led her toward the store. "Come on. I'll introduce you to Miranda Merrick. She used to act on Broadway until she got tired of the pace of life and moved to Losthampton."

Miranda was a tall, elegant redhead, perhaps in her late forties, who moved as though she was center stage. He heard China groan as Miranda spotted them from across the store and started toward them.

"Good grief," she said under her breath to Campbell. "Another woman from the Karen Benning school of grace and beauty. Don't try to tell me you're not into redheads. Don't you know any plain women?"

"I wasn't aware there was any such thing." He raised his voice. "Miranda, I'd like you to meet a friend of mine."

Despite China's complaint about Miranda's knock-out looks, she was gracious and warm and told Miranda about her shopping service in Southern California.

When Campbell left them, they were talking Holly-wood-waist pants and ballerina necklines and all sorts of other foreign terms that made him eager to escape. He excused himself, told China he'd meet her at one o'clock under the weather-and-temperature sign on the bank. He pointed across the street to show her where it was. "And Clifford's is one block up from here on the corner."

She thanked him as Miranda led her toward another part of the store.

He expelled a sigh of relief as he walked into Di-Mello's Marine and Auto Parts. It was loud with the shriek of air compressors and male voices. It smelled of rubber and motor oil, but at least he could identify all the products sold here.

He paid for Daniel's order and was just walking out of the store when Brian walked in. Brian carried a small outboard motor and looked troubled. Campbell had to catch his arm to be noticed.

"Brian," he said when Brian finally looked up at him. His eyes were red rimmed, as though he hadn't slept. "Something wrong?"

Brian smiled thinly. "Hi, Cam. Yeah. The store was broken into last night. Somebody did a lot of damage, broke open jars of food and dumped them all over, stove in the bottom of half of the boats before the lady who lives across the road heard the noise and called the police. They called me about three-thirty this morning and asked me to come down and assess the damage."

Campbell felt the stirrings of anger. "Your father?" he asked. Corbin Girard had been very vocal about his resentment of Brian's attachment to the Abbotts.

"I went right over to his place when I saw what had happened," Brian said with a shrug of confusion, "but he hasn't been in residence for more than a week."

"I wouldn't put it past him to hire it done."

"Yeah, but for what purpose? He's disowned me. He's fired me from the company. I can't believe he'd want to destroy my dinky little store and my canoe and rowboat flotilla." The boat-rental part of his business did have a motley collection of boats, but he kept them in good working condition, and did a fairly brisk business. "I'm guessing it was kids with nothing else to do."

Maybe, Campbell thought. But there'd been little of that sort of malicious damage in Losthampton over the years.

"Well," he asked, "why didn't you call me?"

Brian shrugged. "Didn't the family leave this morning? I intended to come by and wave them off with you, but I was still talking to the police. I came to town to get some cleaning supplies and to see if this motor can be repaired. The boat's in good shape, but I think they put sugar in this."

Campbell glanced at his watch. "Let me come back with you and help you clean up."

"No, no. I—"

"I'm here with China, but I'm not supposed to pick her up until one for lunch. Let me find her and tell her what's going on. I'll come back to take her to lunch, then drop her home and finish helping you clean up."

"It's not your—"

"You got the cleaning stuff yet?"

"Yeah, but I—"

"Well, get the motor and let's get moving. You can come back to town with me at one and we'll all have lunch."

Brian sighed and frowned at him. "Do you ever stop to listen to what someone else has to say?"

"Only if I want to hear it."

"Might I remind you that I'm older than you are?"

"Oh, please. I don't treat Killian or Sawyer with any deference. You don't really think I'm going to show you any, do you? Besides, my part of the family isn't really related to you, so the older-brother code doesn't even apply."

"Then why do you want to help me clean up?"

"Because I'm trying to convince China that I'm a gentleman."

"Whoa." Brian looked doubtful. "She doesn't even like you."

"Thanks for pointing that out. Actually, I'm making small strides in that direction. Now, are you going to ask about that outboard, or are we just going to stand here in the doorway and chat?"

Brian gave him a quick, threatening glance. "All right, all right. You go talk to her and I'll meet you back at my place."

"Good."

Campbell found China in Clifford's in the toiletries aisle. He stopped in surprise at the end of the aisle when he saw the number of packages clustered at her feet, the large paper shopping bag dangling from her arm, the cardboard tube clutched in her elbow like a casually held lance.

She looked up from her perusal of a jar of something and saw him. She smiled in surprise, then glanced guiltily at her watch, obviously concluding she was late for their rendezvous.

"No, I'm early," he said quickly, going toward her. He was assailed by a host of feminine fragrances wafting from the items on the shelf. Moisturizers, the overhead sign read. "I just ran into Brian."

She must have seen something in his eyes that made her frown. "What happened? Is he okay?"

"He's fine, but his store was broken into last night and trashed. Apparently they vandalized everything, including the boats. I'm going to go help him clean up, but I'll be back in time to take you to lunch. Then I'll drop you home—"

"Wait." She put the jar back on the shelf. "I've found a lot of what I came for. I'll come along and help."

"In that dress? No, it's messy work."

She was picking up packages off the floor and stuffing them into his arms. "He must have an old shirt I can put on over my dress. Can you manage all that?"

His arms were filled. "Yeah, but how did you have time to buy so much?"

She gave him a superior look while hooking the shopping bag over her arm. "I'm a professional, remember? And while you think there are no advantages to that skill on an estate, it's very useful in other situations." She began walking toward the doors.

He followed her. "But I promised you lunch."

"Besides a matching bra and panties set, a new nightgown, a white sweater, and a ridiculously expensive beaded bustier that Miranda was putting on the mark-down table, you're holding a dozen doughnuts and a pound of Godiva chocolates. If that doesn't do it, we can have pizza delivered or something."

When they reached the car, he was unable to get a hand free to retrieve his keys. "Right-side pocket," he told her.

She put a package down on the hood to delve gently into his pants pocket. Shoppers wandered by, the women smiling at his overburdened state, the men appreciating vicariously the thrill of having a woman explore his pocket.

He returned their smiles, pretending to be unaffected as China's fingers moved against his hipbone, then had to go deeper to locate the keys. He had to admit that for all the exasperations and aggravations of the past month, life had its sweet moments.

She found the keys too quickly, held them up with a "ta-da" of victory, apparently unmindful of the delicious agonies she'd caused him. She opened the trunk, tossed her packages into it, then handed him the keys. Within seconds she was sitting in the front passenger seat, clearly eager to help Brian.

"You're very fond of Brian," he said, fishing, as he pulled out into the busy street.

"Yes," she admitted. He felt her attention as he kept his eyes on the road. "You are, too."

"He's my brother."

"Technically, he isn't."

"Who lives by 'technically'? He's a good guy, he saved Sawyer's life, and I like him."

"He treated me like a human being," she said, "when you couldn't stand the sight of me. That's why I like him."

Campbell was finally clear of the busy downtown streets and accelerated. With a straight stretch ahead for several blocks, he glanced her way. "The sight of you was never a problem."

"Don't be nice," she advised, backhanding him on the arm. "I'll begin to think I was picked up by a stranger."

She was apparently not receptive to his subtle search for an answer about her feelings for Brian. "I'm trying to determine," he said plainly, "if you're…romantically inclined toward Brian."

Her reply was quick and sounded firm. "No, I'm not. I'm not romantically inclined, period. I need focus, remember?"

Okay, that was good. Though she'd seen a lot of Brian over the past month, she wasn't falling for him. And though she might think she didn't have any romantic feelings, she was very much mistaken. Her kisses had made that clear.

All in all, not a bad position in which to find himself.

BRIAN'S SHOP WAS much more of a mess than China had imagined. Gooey liquids—condiments, jarred soups, soda, cleaning agents and other things she couldn't even identify—had been slopped together in a pungent ooze that made walking on the old plank floor treacherous.

One window had been smashed, several light fixtures broken, the door pulled off a freezer so that everything it contained, from ice cream to frozen dinners, was spoiled and contributing to a ripeness in the air.

"I vote that we get the worst of it up," Campbell suggested bracingly, "and call a cleaning service."

"Already did that." Brian, who'd arrived about the same time they did, took several careful steps into the shop and placed his purchases on a shelf whose contents had been swept onto the floor last night. "They're coming tomorrow. You guys really don't have to do this."

"Sure we do." China tossed her purse at the shelf. "Do you have an old shirt or an apron I can wear?"

He moved carefully toward an elegant oak wardrobe in the back that was remarkably unscathed. China remembered that it was where he kept Losthampton T-shirts and sweatshirts and other souvenirs.

He grabbed something off the shelf and brought it back to her. "How about these flannel pjs?"

She opened them out. They were dark blue and decorated with stars and crescent moons.

"The back room's not too bad. You can use it to change."

"Okay." She started to pick her way back and uttered a little scream of surprise when she was suddenly swept up into Campbell's arms. "What about those white shoes?" he asked as he carried her to the back.

"They're canvas. They go in the washer," she said, hoping she didn't sound as breathless as she felt. She was sharply aware of every single place his fingertips connected with her body, primarily on her thigh.

Great. So much for focus.

But he put her down unceremoniously in the back and pulled the curtain that separated the back from the front, then returned to Brian. "What do you say we move all the racks out onto the porch," she heard him ask, "since the floor's going to have to be done by the cleaning crew, anyway, and that'll make it easier to get all the junk up?"

"Sure," Brian replied. "I started scraping stuff into buckets this morning, but gave myself a break to go to town."

"You're to be commended," Campbell said. "I wouldn't have come back. Let's start with this one."

China heard heaving and grunting as she placed her dress over the back of a chair and pulled on the pajamas. They were several sizes too big, but she cuffed the arms and legs and folded over the waist, holding it in place with a big paper clip from Brian's desk.

She found a dustpan and a bucket in a small tool closet. While the men moved out the shelving, she used the dustpan like a scoop and gathered broken glass and muck into the bucket. For an hour she scooped and carried the bucket out to the Dumpster.

With all the shelves finally moved out, Campbell and Brian found floor brushes and buckets and did the same.

"China, why don't you stop and make some coffee," Campbell called to her from across the shop.

"*You* stop and make coffee," she replied, knowing he was trying to give her a break but happy with the progress she was making.

Bent over a particularly messy bucket to which she was adding another scoop of gunk, she didn't see him coming. He hooked an arm around her waist, lifted her off the floor and carried her against his side to the back wall where Brian had a shelf set up with a coffeepot, cups and coffee.

"Will you stop *doing* that?" she demanded as he set her on her feet. She made a production of brushing off her pajamas to hide the fact that she could still feel his hands everywhere.

"If you'll just do what I ask. Where are the doughnuts?"

"In the back of the car." She folded her arms. "Why can't you make the coffee?"

"Because you do a better job." He took a handkerchief from his pocket and swiped it across her cheek. "If I have to make the coffee, I get to kiss you again."

Wouldn't he be surprised to know that was not the deterrent he thought it was. "Fine," she said, righting the overturned coffeepot. Fortunately it seemed to be intact. "But the strawberry-cream cheese croissant is mine. What are we going to do for cups?"

Two coffee cups had been smashed on the floor right where she stood. "I've got a couple in the back," Brian said, pushing Campbell toward the door. "Go get the doughnuts. If she runs off because you threatened to kiss her, we'll never get this place cleaned up."

Minutes later they were sitting on the floor in the back room, praising themselves for eradicating much of the mess in such a short time. Brian and Campbell put away three or four doughnuts—she lost count—while she enjoyed a second croissant.

Afterward, Campbell helped Brian take an inventory so that he could reorder food and supplies, and China took down the soiled curtains, washed the remaining window, and the mirrors in the dressing room—miraculously unbroken, along with the small-paned windows in the back door.

As they continued to prepare an order, she busied herself with little jobs she thought might help. She sharpened the pencils on Brian's desk, refilled the coffee canister from a tin she found in the back, washed the cups they'd used and set them on the shelf.

Before she knew it, the sun was low in the sky and Campbell was walking into the back room with a fragrant pizza. Brian followed with a bottle of soda and a fistful of napkins.

She couldn't believe she had an appetite after having eaten the two croissants for lunch, but they'd all worked long and hard enough to make them hungry.

Brian put the cushion from his chair on the floor for China, and they all sprawled out again to eat.

"Campbell had a decorator come by today," China said to Brian. "Chloe wants her to add a room for you at Shepherd's Knoll."

Brian looked up from sprinkling his pizza with red pepper. "Well, that's thoughtful, but hardly necessary. I mean, I'm only a mile away."

"She thinks it would be nice if you had a place to stay with the family on holidays and, you know, family occasions."

Brian appeared touched and momentarily speechless. Not wanting him to be uncomfortable, China kept talking. "Between your bedroom and bath, there's a fireplace that can be enjoyed from either room. How's that for elegance?"

Campbell pretended hurt feelings. "The rest of us

have to make do with a wall heater, while your suite has definite babe-magnet properties."

Brian grinned. "Then you can feel free to use it when I'm not there. Some of us don't need babe-magnet tricks."

"Oh, yeah," Campbell drawled. "You look so cool in your ketchup- and chocolate-syrup-stained jeans."

Brian and Campbell started relating stories about their childhood—when they competed in sports before they knew they were related. Full of pizza and soda, China reclined on her side with an elbow on the pillow to support her head, intending to give them her full attention. But soon her head was too heavy for her hand and she rested it on the pillow for a moment—then drifted off to the warm sounds of their shared memories and their laughter.

When she awoke it was dusk, and cool salty air rippled over her body. Campbell was carrying her yet again. She was too tired to fuss.

"What happened this time?" she asked lazily. "I don't remember arguing with you."

"Time to go home," he said. Brian opened the passenger door and Campbell placed her inside. "It was carry you or let you spend the night on the back-room floor. I didn't think you'd want that."

"You are so insightful." She lifted her very heavy arm to allow him to put the seat belt around her.

Brian leaned into the car and kissed her cheek. "Thanks for all the help, China. I owe you two a fabulous dinner sometime soon."

She smiled sleepily. "Nah. Happy to help. That's what siblings are for."

He laughed. "But none of us is really related."

"We decided that doesn't matter. We're sort of like an urban tribe, even though we're in the suburbs."

Campbell climbed in behind the wheel and Brian reached across China to grip his shoulder. "Thanks, Cam. I appreciate all you did."

"Not a problem. I'll come back tomorrow on the chance there's something else you need."

"I'll call you if I need you."

"I don't trust you. I'll come by."

Campbell drove off into the encroaching darkness, and China tried to wake up but didn't seem quite able to focus her energy. Instead, she slipped deeper into warm sleep. Focus, she realized as she lost awareness again, was becoming a big problem for her.

Chapter Eight

China awoke to velvety darkness and the warm comfort of her bed at Shepherd's Knoll. The last thing she remembered was being in Campbell's car and feeling sleepy, a sense of rightness and security cocooning her.

He must have carried her in from the car and up the stairs. She felt deprived at not remembering that.

Wide-awake now, she pulled on a blue-and-white cotton robe over her white slip-nightie and went down to the kitchen to make a cup of tea. She turned on only the small lamp at a desk in the corner, which Kezia used to prepare menus. She filled the kettle at the sink and was about to put it on the stove when she spotted a flicker of light in the part of the orchard where the vintage trees were.

What on earth…? As she watched, the flicker grew to a glow and quickly to visible flame.

She put the kettle down and stared, unable to believe her eyes. Then her heart sank. The Duchess!

"Campbell!" she shouted even as she snatched the flashlight from its charger on a hook by the back door and raced out into the night. The security lights lit her path part of the way, but as she ran beyond them and the shadows swallowed her, she turned on the flashlight and kept running. To her left was the burning tree, and to her right, scurrying movements in the other trees and the sounds of urgent conversation.

She was torn between running for the water hose and trying to stop whoever had done this. Anger superseded common sense, and she flashed her light toward the movement, shouting promises of retribution.

"What do you think you're doing!" she demanded, realizing, as she heard her own words, how stupid a question that was. They thought they were setting fire to the vintage section of the Abbotts' orchard. And they were.

Why didn't really matter at the moment, except that it was so cruel and reprehensible an act, and she'd so grown to love this orchard, particularly the old trees, that she operated on emotion rather than caution.

She heard a rustling to her right and ran into the trees in pursuit of it. Something struck the trunk of a tree right beside her, then ricocheted sharply off the side of her head. "Ow!" she wailed, as awareness fell away and she sank into blurring darkness.

CAMPBELL HEARD the crack of sound, followed by an expression of pain. He was certain it was China's voice.

He'd been awakened by her shout of his name, looked out his window and seen the fire. Then he'd caught sight of her running form picked out by a spotlight. He'd raised the window and called her name, telling her to come back, but she didn't hear him. Or, knowing her, she'd heard him and ignored him.

He yanked on his jeans over the briefs and T-shirt he wore to bed and ran down the stairs and out the back door, shouting for Winfield. He heard him behind him now, thumping over the ground.

Campbell had been heading for the fire, but at the sound of China's voice, he turned in that direction, fear seizing him, making it suddenly difficult to breathe.

"China!" he cried.

He stopped to listen. There was no response but the sound of running feet. Then he heard a small, faint sound.

"Cam?" The frail voice came from somewhere behind him.

Winfield raced past him in pursuit of the running feet, and Campbell backtracked toward the sound till he caught a faint glow of light.

He found China sitting up against a tree, rubbing her head, a flashlight on the ground at her side. He got down on his knees beside her, alarmed by the feeble sound of her voice and the trickle of blood near her ear.

"Something hit me," she said as he tried to part her disheveled hair to assess the damage. He brushed her interfering hand aside and held the flashlight up.

A score of recriminations sat on the tip of his tongue, but he held them back. He'd been both horrified and admiring of her fearless race toward the fire.

"It's never smart to chase an enemy you can't see," he said. The wound wasn't deep, but a formidable bump was already taking shape on her scalp. He dabbed at the blood with the hem of his T-shirt. "You okay? I want you to just sit here while I put the fire out."

"I'll help...." She tried to get to her feet.

He pushed on her shoulder. "No. Stay here. Hold the light."

He went for the hose, but Winfield was already running toward the Duchess with it. Wood had been stacked at the base of the tree, and that seemed to be what was burning. One branch had caught, but the flames on it were doused the moment the water hit it. Straw had been stacked around many of the trees, he noticed, but China's race into the orchard must have stopped the perpetrators before they could set the others alight.

"I've got this," Winfield told him. "Take care of Miss Grant."

She was walking hesitantly toward Campbell, a hand to her head, the flashlight shining in his face. He went to take it from her, then lifted her in his arms.

"Do you *ever* listen?" he asked impatiently, striding in the direction of the house.

"Hard not to," she replied, looping her arms around his neck and leaning her head on his shoulder. "You tend to be rather loud."

"China—"

"Cam, I have a terrible headache."

Now guilt and anger made a mess of his thought processes. "I'm taking you to the hospital. The cut isn't bad, but it must have been quite a blow. You could be concussed."

"I'm fine," she insisted, holding him more tightly.

"Whatever it was that hit me connected with the tree first. I have no double vision, no nausea."

"I didn't realize you had a medical degree…. Why in hell did you run out in the dark?"

They'd reached the floodlit part of the yard and she lifted her head off his shoulder to frown at him. "The Duchess was on fire!"

"After what happened last night at Brian's, didn't it occur to you that someone might have set it?"

"Of course it did." She looked him as though that was a silly question. "I wanted to catch them!"

"You should have waited for me and Winfield."

"I didn't want them to get away."

"Well, they did, and they managed to hurt you first."

She rested her head against him again and heaved a sigh. "I'm not hurt," she said in a small voice. "I just have a headache."

Campbell carried China into the living room, placed her on the big sofa and covered her with one of the throws his mother kept in the base of the coffee table. Daniel and Kezia burst in through the kitchen, Kezia belting her robe and Daniel carrying a rifle that usually decorated the wall of his den.

"What's going on?" Daniel asked worriedly. "We saw fire, then saw you carrying China back from the orchard."

Kezia spotted her on the sofa and went to her as Campbell explained what had happened. Daniel hurried out to help Winfield as Campbell called Dr. Doyle, then the police.

After speaking with China, Winfield, then Campbell, the police concluded that the vandalism was probably the work of bored teens.

"But they knocked China unconscious," Campbell argued. "That doesn't sound like kids, does it?" Then he added, "Last night, my brother's place was broken into. The general store and boat rental."

David Draper, the older of the two officers and an acquaintance of Sawyer's, looked up. "Brian Girard's place. He's your brother? I didn't know that."

"It's a long story."

"You think someone's targeting your family?" Draper asked.

Campbell was considering that. And he'd wager he knew who it was. But he had no proof to offer. "I'd say it looks that way."

"We'll put your house and the store on our patrol route. Meanwhile, when it's daylight, we'll send someone to walk through the orchard, see if they can find anything that'll help identify whoever did this." The officer handed Campbell a business card as he walked him and his partner to the door.

The doctor told Campbell that China showed no signs of concussion. "Her vitals are normal, she seems perfectly cognitive, no problems with vision or speech or memory. Of course, the trouble with head injuries is that everything can look fine, but a problem can show up later. It'd be a good idea to watch her closely for a day or two." He smiled. "Only problem I see is the one she shares with your mother—an aversion to going to the hospital."

Campbell shook his hand. "I appreciate your coming out in the middle of the night. I'll see that the Abbott Mills Foundation makes a contribution to your inner-city clinic."

"That isn't necessary," the doctor said. "I'm happy to do this for you."

"But it was above and beyond the call." Campbell had always appreciated that, though the man kept his "society" practice going because his father had started it, all his weekend energy went to the establishment of a clinic in the middle of Harlem, and the support of the young doctors who worked in it. "Sawyer will be in touch with you."

"Thank you. If you see any sign of trouble in her, call me right away."

Campbell grinned. "I'm sure you don't mean *any* sign of trouble. Because there are a lot of them."

"Medical trouble," the doctor clarified.

As Campbell walked him out, Daniel returned. "We're going to sit out there the rest of the night. I'm just back for some coffee and a couple of blankets. And Winfield's cell phone. He says it's on his bedside table."

Campbell frowned at Daniel. "Night watchman isn't in your job description."

"I've been a part of this family for a long time," he replied. "You can't assault an Abbott and expect me to stand by. I know China isn't an Abbott, but this whole family's a more complicated conglomerate than Abbott Mills is."

Campbell slapped his shoulder. "Well put, Daniel. Thank you."

While Daniel went upstairs in search of blankets and

Winfield's cell phone, Kezia headed for the kitchen to make coffee.

China was fast asleep on the sofa, her hair in seductive disarray over her face and his mother's favorite brocade pillow. Her throat and part of one arm were bared by the loose cotton robe. Campbell drew up the throw to cover her, wanting to press his lips to the curve of her shoulder but afraid of waking her.

The doctor had said to watch her closely.

Taking her up to his room or hers was too dangerous, considering the state of his nerves and his libido, so it would be best to leave her on the sofa and try to get comfortable on a nearby chair.

He dismissed a Boston rocker and a genuine but very uncomfortable Shaker chair, and decided on the overstuffed one that matched the sofa. It didn't have an ottoman, but if he pulled it up to the end of the sofa, he could rest his feet there.

When Kezia saw what he planned to do, she volunteered to sit up with her, but this was *his* responsibility. China had rushed out foolishly to defend the trees he'd taught her to love as much as he did. Daniel went off with his thermos of coffee to join Winfield, and Campbell insisted that Kezia stay in one of the spare rooms she always kept prepared for company. On the chance there were any more problems tonight, he didn't want her to be alone in the old guest house.

He turned off all the lights except the desk lamp in the kitchen, and settled into the big chair, propping his feet on the sofa. China, curled up in a ball, left him a lot of room.

An Important Message from the Editors

Dear Reader,

If you'd enjoy reading romance novels with larger print that's easier on your eyes, let us send you TWO FREE HARLEQUIN SUPERROMANCE® NOVELS in our NEW LARGER-PRINT EDITION. These books are complete and unabridged, but the type is set about 25% bigger to make it easier to read. Look inside for an actual-size sample.

By the way, you'll also get a surprise gift with your two free books!

Pam Powers

Peel off Seal and Place Inside...

See the
larger-print
difference.

THE RIGHT WOMAN

she'd thought she was fine. It took Daniel's words and Brooke's question to make her realize she was far from a full recovery.

She'd made a start with her sister's help and she intended to go forward now. Sarah felt as if she'd been living in a darkened room and some-one had suddenly opened a door, letting in the fresh air and sunshine. She could feel its warmth slowly seeping into the coldest part of her. The feeling was liberating. She realized it was only a small step and she had a long way to go, but she was ready to face life again with Serena and her family behind her.

All too soon, they were saying goodbye and Sarah experienced a moment of sadness for all the years she and Serena had missed. But they had each other now and that's what She held

Like what you see?
Then send for TWO FREE
larger-print books!

Printed in the U.S.A.
Publisher acknowledges the copyright holder of the excerpt from this individual work as follows:
THE RIGHT WOMAN Copyright © 2004 by Linda Warren. All rights reserved.
® and TM are trademarks owned and used by the trademark owner and/or its licensee.

YOURS FREE!
*You'll get a great mystery gift with
your two free larger-print books!*

GET TWO FREE LARGER-PRINT BOOKS!

YES! Please send me two free Harlequin Superromance® novels in the larger-print edition, and my free mystery gift, too. I understand that I am under no obligation to purchase anything, as explained on the back of this insert.

PLACE FREE GIFTS SEAL HERE

139 HDL D7U5   339 HDL D7U6

FIRST NAME

LAST NAME

ADDRESS

APT.#

CITY

STATE/PROV.

ZIP/POSTAL CODE

Are you a current Harlequin Superromance® subscriber and want to receive the larger-print edition?
Call 1-800-221-5011 today!

Offer limited to one per household. All orders subject to approval. Credit or debit balances in a customer's account(s) may be offset by any other outstanding balance owed by or to the customer.

▼ **DETACH AND MAIL CARD TODAY!** ▼

(H-SLPO-05/05) © 2004 Harlequin Enterprises Ltd.

The Harlequin Reader Service™ — Here's How It Works:

Accepting your 2 free Harlequin Superromance® books and gift places you under no obligation to buy anything. You may keep the books and gift and return the shipping statement marked "cancel." If you do not cancel, about a month later we'll send you 6 additional Harlequin Superromance larger-print books and bill you just $4.94 each in the U.S., or $5.49 each in Canada, plus 25¢ shipping & handling per book and applicable taxes if any.* That's the complete price and — compared to cover prices of $5.75 each in the U.S. and $6.75 each in Canada — it's quite a bargain! You may cancel at any time, but if you choose to continue, every month we'll send you 6 more books, which you may either purchase at the discount price or return to us and cancel your subscription.

*Terms and prices subject to change without notice. Sales tax applicable in N.Y. Canadian residents will be charged applicable provincial taxes and GST.

If offer card is missing write to: Harlequin Reader Service, 3010 Walden Ave., P.O. Box 1867, Buffalo, NY 14240-1867

BUSINESS REPLY MAIL
FIRST-CLASS MAIL   PERMIT NO. 717-003   BUFFALO, NY

POSTAGE WILL BE PAID BY ADDRESSEE

HARLEQUIN READER SERVICE
3010 WALDEN AVE
PO BOX 1867
BUFFALO NY 14240-9952

NO POSTAGE
NECESSARY
IF MAILED
IN THE
UNITED STATES

He was awakened just before dawn by small cries of distress and found China stirring fitfully, in the throes of a nightmare.

"It's burning," she said anxiously, twisting and turning as though trying to toss off the throw. "Burning... burning..."

He sat on the edge of the sofa, shushing her, telling her it was all right, that it was just a nightmare.

She opened her eyes and studied him sleepily. He swept the hair out of her face and pulled up the shoulder of the cursed robe. He wasn't sure if she was awake or not.

"Campbell," she said, wrapping her arms around his middle. "Not my brother."

So, she was awake. "Right," he said.

"Carried me...over the threshold." She leaned into him and snuggled.

Threshold? She was dreaming.

"No, just out of the orchard," he corrected, trying to push her back to the pillow, but she resisted, continuing to hold him.

"Love him," she said, snuggling into him. "Home."

Love him? "China?"

Deep breaths came from her as she fell silent again and slept. He was perched uncomfortably on the edge of the sofa, but she had a grip on him he wasn't going to be able to break without shaking her awake. And if she was dreaming of loving him, he didn't want to do that.

Unwilling to think about what that meant, he lifted her so that he could turn and settle into the corner of the sofa, allowing her to continue to hold him while stretching out her legs. And he could stretch his out to the big chair he'd been sleeping in.

He linked his fingers around her, felt her settle into him with a little sound of contentment, and closed his eyes. Despite his frayed nerves, he still managed to fall asleep.

CHINA WAS AWARE of Campbell's arms around her before she even opened her eyes. She was snugly tucked against him, her right arm hooked around his neck, her cheek pressed into a warm, solid pectoral muscle.

She waited for the clutch of tension that always took her over when he was around. But she felt no tension. She was uncharacteristically relaxed, pleasantly immersed in the rightness of the moment, happy with the possessive quality of his embrace. She'd tried hard to fight it—this wasn't the right time, life was too complicated, too unsure, too…too everything—but all those things didn't seem to matter now.

She tightened her grip on his neck to pull herself up a little higher and opened her eyes. She was not entirely surprised to find him watching her, his dark eyes filled with the same pleasure in the moment she was experiencing.

His fingertips brushed her hair out of her face. Something melted deep inside her.

"What's your name?" he asked. That question puzzled her, then she realized why he'd asked it. It was one of the concussion-test questions.

She didn't want to return to the real world just yet, wanted to linger a little longer in this bubble of intimacy. "If you're going to hold a woman through the night," she said lazily, "you should maybe ask that first."

"Cute. What's your name?"

She stretched an arm languidly. "Oh, I'm known by many names," she said, then wrapped that arm around him. "Angel, Siren, Womankind, Mistress." She thought she was being terribly clever, but he simply continued to wait.

She sighed. "China Lorinda Grant."

"Lorinda?"

"Yes. My mother always said she just liked it."

"Did she tell you where the China comes from?"

"A heroine in a book. A gothic romance, I think."

He held up two fingers. "How many?"

She brushed his hand away and focused on his mouth. "I'm more interested in your lips. Two of them, with the smallest scar—" she touched the corner of his mouth "—right there. What's that from?"

"Skateboarding. I was learning to kick up and catch the board, but I did it with my mouth that particular time." He put a diagnostic hand to her forehead. "No headache?"

"No."

"Vision okay?"

"I'm seeing you very clearly."

"No nausea?"

"Just hunger."

A voice shouted from the kitchen, "If you two are ready to stop canoodling, I'll make you some breakfast!"

China groaned and fell against Campbell's shoulder. "Great. My first attempt at seduction and there's a witness to my failure."

He laughed and kissed her temple. "You didn't fail. I heard her stirring around. You want to give me a hand up? I think I'm paralyzed."

China levered herself off him, then offered her hand and pulled. He held on to her, pushed against the arm of the sofa and got to his feet, wincing and groaning.

When he entered the kitchen, China right behind, he frowned at the stack of dishes on the counter, waiting to go into the dishwasher. "Have Winfield and Daniel come and gone already?" he asked Kezia.

She nodded. "Winfield's acting like he's packing a six-gun. He feels responsible that someone got in last night."

Campbell went to the window to look out on the yard. "Nobody's blaming him. You never know if your security system is effective or not until it's tested, then you adjust accordingly."

"He feels really badly that China got hurt."

"I'm fine," she insisted.

"He wants to call Killian and Sawyer," Kezia added grimly.

Campbell turned away from the window. "Absolutely not. Where is he?"

"I'm right here." Winfield walked in, a clipboard in his hand. "Good morning," he said. "I hope you don't mind that I used your office to make some calls."

"Of course not," Campbell replied. "As long as you didn't call Killian or Sawyer."

"I haven't yet, but I think we should."

"No," Campbell said again. "Killian felt the London issue was important enough that he should be there, and Sawyer hasn't had a break in ages. He deserves this time with Sophie and the kids. And anyway, that'd only upset Mom, and we don't need that."

Kezia brought the coffeepot and cups to the table. "Why don't you all sit down," she suggested, "and I'll get breakfast under way. Winfield, you must be ready for a coffee break, aren't you?"

Winfield nodded, and he and Campbell sat opposite each other. China went for the sugar and cream. Kezia handed her a bowl of fruit, then busied herself chopping onions and cheese for omelets.

"This morning I discovered that the security system had been disabled," Winfield said. "Thanks, China. No fruit for me. I feel fairly sure the vandals aren't just kids, but someone, an adult, with a grudge. And of course, Corbin Girard comes to mind."

Campbell nodded. "Yes. But setting fire to the vintage orchard seems like a relatively small thing to do, considering. I mean, his plan has always been to destroy us financially, but—"

"I think his plan was the big orchard, too, only China woke up and saw the fire."

"Even so, it's still relatively minor destruction."

"True, but let's face it," Winfield said, "the old man's not balanced. And ever since Brian came over to our side, the old man's longtime grudge has been personal. He doesn't want the Abbotts to have one more thing that belongs to him—even though he doesn't want Brian and never did. He knows you put a lot of effort into the orchard, and Shepherd's Knoll gets publicity from it every year at harvest time. It's a big event around here. Only problem is, Girard doesn't seem to be in town. I checked. His staff says he's in Dallas until next week. Of course, he may have lied to them, or *asked* them to lie for him."

Campbell nodded. "Well, we have to deal with what's happening, whatever the reason."

"Exactly. So I've hired some rent-a-cops from the city so that a couple of men are on guard twenty-four hours a day. I also think it'd be a good idea if you stayed close to home."

"I intend to," Campbell said. "But I'm going to Brian's this morning for a couple of hours to help him pull his boats out of the water. I'll try to talk him into staying with us for a few days. He can't open the store until his stock arrives, anyway. If somebody is after us, he shouldn't be out there alone."

"Okay. I can assign a couple of men to watch his place, too. About the harvest," Winfield said. "I've been through this with you only once, so you'll have to refresh my memory. Is it time? You don't hire help for that?"

Campbell shook his head. "Not for the vintage trees, which won't be ready until September. The family usually handles them. It's only twenty-six trees. We hire for the big orchard, but that's later still."

Winfield nodded. "Good. I wasn't looking forward to doing background checks on a lot of people right now."

Campbell turned to China, his estate-manager persona kicking in. "That means no taking off to town by yourself, no wandering off to the beach, no running out in the middle of the night to investigate anything."

After the kind, funny, patient soul mate she'd awakened to, China felt as though she was back at square one. But she understood his concern, and his and Winfield's efforts to keep the house and all its inhabitants safe.

She nodded. "Sure."

He raised an eyebrow, a smile threatening. "No argument?"

"Of course not."

When Kezia served the omelets, Winfield excused himself to arrange transportation for the security guards. He wanted them in place by nightfall.

"You want to come with me to Brian's?" Campbell asked China.

Kezia closed the top of a plastic garbage bag and left the house to take it outside to the shed. Campbell leaned closer. "I thought you might want another shot at that attempt at seduction."

She was beginning to come to her senses about that. Reality had set in since she'd awakened in that wonderfully mellow mood. Even without considering what had happened last night, there was too much upheaval in her life to begin a romance. The moment she heard from Janet, she had to prepare herself to learn whether or not her sister was an Abbott, then she had to take off on her own search for her parents. And Campbell had put a long-awaited job on hold pending the outcome of the Janet-Abigail issue. There was not even time to indulge in a frivolous flirtation.

She had a feeling nothing with Campbell would be frivolous, anyway.

"Seduction loses its impact in daytime," she said,

pretending lightheartedness as she put blueberry jam on her toast. "I'm afraid it'll have to wait."

She hadn't fooled him; she could see that in the amused glance he sent her. "Lost your nerve, huh?"

She avoided his eyes. "It just isn't compatible with sunken-boat retrieval."

"What about if we stop along the way to Brian's?" he said. He was goading her.

"Seduction on the side of a highway? I don't think so."

"The beach grass is pretty high in some places. Or do you need satin sheets and candlelight?"

"First," she said pointedly, "I need a man who doesn't get his kicks by taunting me."

"Sorry. I just don't want you to think you can make excuses for welching on a deal."

She stopped with a forkful of omelet halfway to her mouth. "What deal? We haven't made a deal."

He appeared unconcerned by her denial. "It wasn't written and signed, but there damn well is a deal going on here, and you know it. Had we been alone when you woke up this morning, we'd be in bed now and not giving a damn about breakfast."

He spoke with complete honesty, and while she admired that, she couldn't quite match it. She put the bite of omelet in her mouth to buy time.

"Maybe it was fortuitous that Kezia was up," she said finally. "It would have been a mistake."

Kezia would be back any moment. Campbell leaned even closer to China. "When you get your courage back," he said, his voice very quiet, "I'll show you that making love with me would never be a mistake."

She probably couldn't deny that and be credible, so she whispered, instead, "Life is too complicated at the moment."

"You're intelligent enough to sort it out." He smiled. "And making love with me might clarify a few things for you."

"You're so good," she asked, "that you'll answer the questions of the universe for me?"

He dismissed her sarcasm with a scolding shake of his head. "No. But I'll bet it'll answer a few questions you have about yourself."

Kezia came back into the kitchen, and Campbell went to work on his omelet. China nibbled at her toast, completely unsettled.

She wondered what was wrong with her that she didn't seem to be able to make up her mind about what course her life should follow. Interest in a man was a pretty major thing in a woman's life, but she didn't seem to be able to decide if it should take place in hers.

Well, that wasn't precisely true. It was taking place whether she wanted it to or not. But should she pursue it? Allow him to pursue her? One moment she was sure it was a bad idea, and the next, his kisses and his eyes were so intoxicating she couldn't imagine moving on without him beside her.

But he was going to Florida, and she would have to go to Canada. No. It would never work.

She had to find a way to distance herself from him. But she didn't think anything short of joining the next exploratory mission to Mars would accomplish that.

Chapter Nine

Brian's small fleet of boats were dragged ashore relatively quickly. Young men playing volleyball on the beach became involved in the project and made short work of helping carry the boats to a boatyard a small distance away, where Brian had arranged to have them repaired.

In shorts and T-shirt, China worked as hard as anyone and supported the stern of an overturned canoe while a stalwart young man, one of the volleyball teams' captains, carried the bow. Except for a plea that he "slow down!" as he led the way through the grass to the boatyard, she kept up very well.

Campbell, following them with the bow of a ten-foot dinghy, could see only her shapely calves and trim ankles, and her canvas shoes eating up the ground ahead of him. Still—and despite the heavy work—he was a desperate heap of desire and making every effort to pretend otherwise.

When they dropped the boats in the yard, China straightened from her task, unaware that the water dripping from the boat had soaked the front of her shirt, and a very delicate demi-bra patterned in floral lace was enticingly visible.

The team captain with whom she'd carried a boat, didn't seem able to take his eyes off her. He asked her for a date.

She smiled graciously. "Thanks, but I'm…not available."

Campbell smiled as he unknotted the shirt he'd tied around his waist—he'd stripped it off before picking up the boat. He'd heard this line before, had even used it himself. It made rejection less painful. Now he tossed her his shirt as he helped another team ease their boat to the ground.

China was about to deny that she was cold, when catching the shirt against her chest forced her to look down and recognize the problem. She quickly pulled it on.

"Ah," Campbell heard the team captain say. "So it's him. Well, you know, if you ever get tired of money, looks and brawn, I'm here every summer."

China shook his hand. Then she fell into step beside Campbell as they all walked back to the beach. "You might have told me," she said under her breath, "that my shirt had become transparent!"

"You don't like it when I get bossy," he reminded her, putting an arm around her shoulders and drawing her closer as the path narrowed.

"Yeah, well, I wouldn't have considered, 'China, I can count the flowers on your bra,' bossy. I'd have considered it gentlemanly."

"Ah. There's that issue again."

"Thanks for the shirt."

"Sure."

Brian gave the team captain several bills and told him to take the guys to lunch. They cheered Brian and he thanked them. The captain blew China a kiss.

Campbell had explained to Brian earlier about the fire last night in the orchard, and told him they thought it would be a good idea if he stayed at Shepherd's Knoll until the vandals were caught. He'd agreed. They went with him now to his home, a beautiful old Gothic Revival home his grandfather had built for his grandmother. It was set back from the street, its grounds occupying several acres.

They waited in a cool, cluttered living room while he ran upstairs for a few changes of clothes.

The place had an almost ecclesiastical look on the outside, but was full of all sorts of secular vanities inside—opulent upholstery and furniture scarves, exotic statuary, high stained-glass windows, even a bearskin rug. There were several potted palms and a fan with bamboo paddles hanging from the center of the ceiling.

"How wonderful," China said, walking around the room, studying old photographs and paintings that adorned the walls. While she looked, Campbell went from window to window, closing and locking them, making sure the back door was secure, closing the door to the basement.

"It's hard to believe a horrible person used to live here." China touched the glossy frond of a palm. "It has such a charming, tropical hotel sort of look."

"Brian's father's place is on the other side of town,"

Campbell corrected her. "This was Brian's paternal grandmother's home. I didn't know her, but she and Corbin weren't on speaking terms, so she had to be a good judge of character."

"Must be hard to have people you hate, or who hate you, in your family. Mine were generally very loving. My mother had a couple of sisters, and they were very close." She stopped her perusal of the room to smile at him. "Like you and your brothers. You don't agree on everything, but you care about each other very much. And you've all held Abby's safe return in your hearts. I don't know what I'd do without Janet."

She'd once felt so deprived that she wasn't an Abbott. But now that her feelings for Campbell had erupted as something decidedly nonfraternal, she felt relieved. Not that she would do anything about it. There was too much about her own life that had to be resolved. But when she left Shepherd's Knoll and went in search of answers, she was sure the love she felt for him would help sustain her.

Brian appeared, a sports bag in hand. "Let me just lock the back door," he said, heading for the kitchen.

"Already did it," Campbell said.

Brian noted the closed windows. He grinned at Campbell. "Kid brothers are supposed to be a nuisance."

"Oh, he can be," China put in with a sweet smile in Campbell's direction. "Give him time."

Brian barked a laugh as Campbell chased her out the door.

AFTER DINNER, China disappeared upstairs to her room and Brian and Daniel watched the Mets game on television. Campbell left the house to meet the men Winfield had hired to stand guard outside the property. They were posted so that one stood in each direction, with two to watch the orchard.

"I'd planned originally on four," Winfield said, "but too much of the orchard's obstructed for one man to watch. So two more men are just going to walk a beat through it."

"Good."

Three of the men were very young, probably younger than Campbell, and three were in their late thirties or early forties, tough-looking veterans of other such duties. Campbell introduced himself to each one, explained what had happened last night, and told them he was grateful for their service and that they would be well compensated.

Winfield nodded his agreement, then clapped Campbell on the shoulder. "Abbotts are a good family to work for."

Campbell went back into the house, pleased with Winfield's work. He found China in the kitchen, helping Kezia put away the ton of groceries she'd bought that afternoon. With six extra staff on two shifts, she needed more provisions.

"Still no word from Janet," China reported. "I just called the inn to make sure they didn't forget to pass on my message. She's apparently not back from her trip yet."

"You think that means she's found something?" he asked. He tried to read her expression to see if the possibility that her sister was making discoveries, about what was in all probability China's life, upset or intrigued her. But it was hard to tell. She'd been guarded this evening, seemed troubled.

"I don't know. I just have to wait and see."

He couldn't dispute that. "Can I do anything to help so the two of you can quit for the day? You've been at this since the wee hours, Kezia."

She put a hand to her forehead and said teasingly with a long-suffering sigh, "Well, that's how it is when you're employed by a big house. It's work, work, work. And there doesn't seem to be anything like a slaves' union that I'm aware of."

"Fortunately you work, work, work for a benevolent master," Campbell laughed. "Just leave out whatever isn't perishable, and put it away tomorrow."

"No, I have to make sandwiches to deliver to Winfield's men. Thanks to China's help, I'm almost finished here. You can go watch the game without guilt." She pushed him toward the doorway to the living room. China had turned her back and was putting canned goods in a cupboard.

He'd give away his inheritance to have back the woman who'd awakened in his arms that morning with a languorous smile and a mind set on seduction. But she'd apparently been thinking again about all the unanswered questions that lay between them.

He knew they existed, but they didn't present a barrier for him. His whole life had been about the unanswered question of where Abby was. He knew how to live around the things for which there seemed to be no answer or solution.

But she was an organized woman who felt she had

to put her life in order before she could go on with it. He should honor that.

Or not.

After he made sure Brian had everything he needed, it was almost midnight. He knew China had gone to bed earlier and that Winfield had picked up the sandwiches for the men outside. Every precaution had been taken and everyone was secure.

He sat at the window for a while, looking out, and saw the moving shadow of the man patrolling this side of the house. Then he paced for a while, wondering how his brothers were doing—if Killian was solving the customer problem, and if Sawyer was having a good time with Sophie's relatives. He thought about his mother, trying to distract herself from the tension of waiting to meet China's sister, the potential Abby.

Chloe was probably doing fine. She loved meeting new people and was at her charming best in a crowd, particularly one that involved family. And Tante Bijou was well enough to be with her, so everything she needed to feel secure was in place.

He peeled down to his underwear and climbed into bed, thinking it was strange to be worrying about the family. That was usually Killian's job. But these were strange times.

He lay still and made an effort to clear his mind, but it simply wouldn't happen. Concerns ran across it like the crawl line on a news program, looped to start over again when it was finished.

He turned onto his stomach and put the pillow over his head. Without sight and sound, his brain finally began to quiet. Slowly, layer after layer, concerns began to leave him. Worries for China and the other members of the household began to slip away.

He was just easing from relaxation into sleep when he felt the touch of something cold on his shoulder. Every instinct for self-protection and the protection of those in his care rose out of him like a rocket. He spun around, flinging his right arm in an arc to catch whoever was behind him and drop them to the mattress.

As he landed on the intruder like a dog on a ball, planting his forearm on a throat, he heard a gasp of alarm, then felt the swipe of silky hair against his cheek—hair with a disturbingly familiar fragrance.

"China?" he asked in disbelief.

"Yeah," she replied in a strangled voice.

As he bit back several bad words, he noticed a few other things about the body under his that had become familiar. Small round breasts were flattened against his chest, and shapely knees dug into his thighs. And in between, a softness he'd dreamed about in just this position.

He rolled off her and onto his side with a groan. "Why in hell didn't you knock?" he asked.

In the darkness, he saw her hand flutter to her throat. She drew a breath and he saw her pale breasts rise and fall. What was she wearing? Or not wearing?

"If you were asleep," she said in a husky whisper, "I didn't want to wake you."

"You touched me."

"To see if you were awake."

He sat up cross-legged, feeling as though he couldn't

get air. She seemed to be having the same difficulty judging by the rise and fall of her chest.

"Okay, I'm awake," he said. "Are you okay?" He wanted to touch her but was afraid to. The moment was rife with an emotional danger that had taken him completely by surprise.

She sat up slowly, coughing, and turned to face him, also sitting cross-legged. "Yes. I'm sorry I alarmed you. I…just wanted to talk."

That was disappointing news, but he didn't really think she'd come to his room to finish what she'd started that morning. Although it would have restored his faith in prayer.

"It's all right. What did you want to talk about?"

"Us."

He couldn't decide if that was good or bad. But considering the way his luck was running…

"What about us?" he asked. "Do you want a light on?"

"No." She sighed and ran a hand through her hair, which was almost invisible in the darkness. "I'm ashamed about this morning."

That didn't make sense. "When this morning?"

"When I woke up. The whole seduction thing." Her hands gestured nervously. "I felt secure in your arms and like everything was right and…maybe because it's what I've wanted since I found out I'm not your sister. But…it wasn't fair."

"To whom?"

"To you. I let you think that we could…that I could…that there was a way this might all work out."

He felt suddenly very testy. "You *let* me think it could

work out? Much as you'd like to control everything, China, you aren't in charge of what I think. Haven't you been paying attention? I had the hots for you long before you woke up this morning with the idea of seducing me." Even in the shadowy room, he saw her try to frost him with a stare.

"What I feel is more than simple *hots*."

She said the word with disdain, apparently unaware that to men the word was almost sacred on some very elemental level. "Well, then, what is it you had in mind this morning? You don't want to talk about love, you don't want me to kiss you, yet you were going for me in a very straightforward manner."

She untangled her legs and put one foot on the floor, clearly intending to leave. "I don't know why I thought I could reason with you," she said huffily, trying to stand.

He caught her arm and pulled her back. "Did you really come here to reason with me? Or do you want something else?"

She yanked her arm out of his hold. "I came to tell you that I care about you…a lot!…but I have other things to do before I can pursue that. I forgot that this morning because I do care a lot, and I'm sorry if I seem to keep changing my mind. But I have no idea what I'm doing, so I can't expect you to be able to figure it out."

She looked upset but he felt merciless. He was on the brink of learning an important truth here and he had to push on. "Okay, I've got that. You've told me that several times. What made you feel you had to come to my room in the middle of the night and tell me again?"

Her eyes flashed. "Because you don't ever listen to

me! I have told you over and over, and yet you keep touching or kissing me and…fussing."

He didn't know whether to take exception to that or not. "Fussing?"

She shrugged a slender shoulder in what he could see, now that his eyes were adjusting to the darkness, was a plain white T-shirt. In the shadows, the white cotton embraced her breasts, showed off her nipples. He was going to die from wanting her.

"Being thoughtful," she interpreted, "protective, sympathetic."

"Ah. And you don't want me to do that anymore?"

It was a simple question. He wasn't quite sure why her face crumpled when he asked it. "No," she said finally, sniffing. "Because I have to go to Canada."

He braced himself to argue this issue again. He understood, of course, how important it was to her. "Right, but I don't get why that has to prevent us from loving each other. Whatever you discover isn't going to change the way I feel about you. And I don't see how it could change what you feel for me."

"It would never change that," she said.

She spoke with such sincerity that he felt a glimmer of hope for the first time in this conversation. She folded her arms, pushing her breasts more tightly into the cotton. He had to look at her face to concentrate. It was pale and forlorn, but he hardened himself against it to get through this.

"When I was a teen, I used to wonder why other adopted kids did searches to find their parents. I thought that if my birth parents hadn't wanted me, then I didn't want them. Of course, I didn't really have that problem, because I was told that my mother died. Then…when Janet and I found the boxes, I…" She shook her head, a pleat appearing between her eyebrows. "I thought I'd been kidnapped, but the contents of Janet's box suggested she'd been left at a hospital. I felt sorry for her, because that meant someone had just given her up. The one person in the whole world who's supposed to love you no matter what had taken her to a hospital and dumped her. But I was stolen. No rejection there, just probably a real longing to have me back."

She was losing control, he could hear it in her voice. He caught her arms and, untangling his legs, pulled her close so that her back was to his chest and he could wrap his arms around her.

"I told her that if I was her, I wouldn't go looking for them," she said, beginning to cry.

He put his cheek to hers and began to rock her gently. "And now it looks like that's *your* story," he said, "and not hers."

She nodded, wrapping her arms around his and weeping.

"China," he chided softly, "you know there are all kinds of reasons a parent leaves a child—death, depression, illness, finances—none of which is selfish. Some of us are better equipped than others to handle hard times, and you can't judge unless you know what they've been through."

"I'm just afraid," she said, swiping a hand at her eyes, "that if I find out I was carelessly abandoned, I'll be angry for the rest of my life. And I wouldn't want anyone to have to share that."

He tightened his grip on her. "That isn't you at all. And whatever you find out about your parents has very little to do with the real you. You grew up without them, and you loved your adopted parents, who you say were kind and generous. If fate saved you from being raised by careless parents, you have every reason to be grateful rather than angry. There are probably lots of kids who'd happily change places with you."

She nodded, drawing a deep breath and pulling herself together. "I know. I just used to imagine that they'd left me because my father died in some UN peacekeeping action, and my mother learned she had some incurable disease. Or they died together in a plane crash hurrying home for my first birthday."

"That could be what happened," he said. "You don't know. But if you're going to go to Canada, you have to be ready to learn that maybe it wasn't anything like that. Maybe your parents were careless or selfish or even self-destructive. But you're who you became without being affected by them in any way except genetically."

"But DNA is such a big thing. It'll determine whether Janet belongs here or not. It determined that I don't, remember?"

"If *you* remember," he corrected, "your DNA determined that you don't, but your personality, your sweetness, your character, made everyone else here want you to stay."

She leaned heavily against him. "I'm sorry I woke you. I should go before someone discovers I'm here."

"There's no one around to care if you are or not. Why don't you stay?"

She turned her face on his shoulder to look up at him.

"Just to sleep," he assured her. "Then if you decide there's something else you want to tell me, you won't scare me to death by walking in on me."

"This wasn't even what I wanted to talk about," she said in a sort of surprised wariness. "I…just wanted to tell you we can't…"

"Yeah, yeah, yeah," he said, stepping out from behind her so that she could stretch out. He fluffed the pillows on the far side. "We can talk about that later."

She smiled up at him from the middle of his bed. "You're saying we should spend the night together first, then talk about how we can't be together?"

He punched his own pillows. "If you try to think things through at night when you're tired, they never seem to make sense."

She crawled to the other side of the bed and got under the covers. "You're the one who doesn't make sense," she grumbled good-naturedly.

He climbed into bed, careful to leave a respectable distance between them. "Go to sleep," he advised.

"Do you ever get up and raid the refrigerator?" she asked as she snuggled down.

"Occasionally. Is that what you were doing last night?"

"No, I was just making tea. But I saw Kezia put lots of good stuff in there to feed the security guys. Bologna and pepper-jack cheese."

He turned his head to look at her. There was something wondrous about seeing her dark head on the neighboring pillow.

"That's not very sophisticated."

"I don't care. I love a bologna-and-pepper-jack sandwich. Grilled. Yum."

"I'm not getting up to make you one, so go to sleep."

She made a disgruntled sound. "I didn't mean you have to stop fussing altogether."

Chapter Ten

China dreamed of babies, fires, a small army marching around the house. She tried to row across a body of water, but her boat had a hole in the bottom and began to sink. Though she tried to scream for help, she couldn't make a sound. When the water reached her chin, she tried to swim, but there was something heavy tied to her back and it dragged her down. She tried to shake it off, but it felt permanently affixed. As panic and desperation overtook her, she made one last, heroic effort to rise out of the water…and sat up, wide-awake.

Her heart thudded and every nerve ending in her body tingled in awareness.

Campbell sat up beside her. He put a hand to her back in comfort, then just as quickly withdrew it. "What'd you dream about?" he asked gently.

"Um…drowning," she said. Oh, God. She had that same feeling she'd awakened with yesterday morning. A need to connect with him, to *know* him in a way that was going to relieve this hideous tension and hopefully help her know which way to turn in her life.

"Well, that's no surprise. You feel overwhelmed. As though you're drowning. It's just your subconscious trying to clarify your waking thoughts for you."

He was being strangely pedantic. She'd much preferred that instant of his comforting hand than she did this explanation of what she already knew. But she thought she understood what he was doing. The air was thick with their feelings for each other and her conviction that there was no time for them.

Still, they sat inches from each other, his shoulder invitingly close to her chin. She appreciated his respect for her feelings when he probably knew he could erase her concerns with one small touch.

She absorbed the moment and admitted to herself in the quiet predawn darkness, *I love him.*

And then she suddenly understood the burden she couldn't shake in her dream, the weight that resulted in her drowning. It was the love she wouldn't admit.

Now that she'd done it—at least to herself—she felt lighter than helium. The notion of loving Campbell filled every little corner, every extremity of her being. She was a feather, a dragon kite, a Macy's Thanksgiving Day Parade balloon.

A laugh escaped her at the feeling of absolute freedom. "I love you," she said aloud.

The was a minute of pulsing silence. Her heart picked up the beat. Oh, no. He wasn't going to respond.

"Pardon me?" he said finally. He didn't move a muscle.

She was surprised by how much courage it took to say the words again. But she did. "I love you."

He made a frustrated sound and climbed out of bed. "Now?" he demanded in a whisper. "In the middle of the night?"

"Well…I think I'll love you when it's daylight, too," she replied, alarmed by his vehemence.

He went to the window, arms helplessly outspread. He made a wonderful picture—white cotton over broad and well-defined shoulders and pecs, lean hips. "No, I mean…I love you, too, but you don't want to do anything about it until you know your background, so it's not really smart to throw the words around in the middle of the night when we're sharing a bed and I'm…I'm…"

"I love you," she repeated, "and I want to make love with you." She stretched a hand out toward him.

He came back to the bed, both hands on the hips of his briefs. "I don't understand."

She dropped her hand to the mattress, exasperated. "You know," she said, annoyed and a little embarrassed, "the mattress mambo, the horizontal—"

"Stop it. An hour ago, you came in here to explain to me why we can't have a relationship, and now, after a dream about drowning, all your doubts are erased?"

She had a sudden, demoralizing clue about why he was behaving this way. "Are you afraid of making love with me now that we've come to it?" she asked. "You think it might change things? That it won't be so easy for you to leave when the time comes?"

"No," he replied gravely. "I'm afraid you've just changed your mind and you might change it back—because you keep doing that. You don't know what you want. You woke up from a bad dream and you need…reassurance. But when it's daylight, you're going to regret it…."

She got up on her knees on the mattress, wishing she had something to throw at him besides a pillow. "I don't use lovemaking to make me feel secure, and I am not going to change my mind again, because I've finally just had the guts to admit my love for you to myself." She was speaking loudly, but she didn't care. "I could tell you I had feelings for you, I could tell you that I cared for you, but saying *I love you* took a lot of guts, and if you can't appreciate that…"

She stepped off the bed and headed for the door.

"Wait," he said from somewhere behind her.

She ignored him and yanked open the door.

He caught her arm, pulled her away from it and closed the door quietly.

She slapped at his bare shoulder. "Don't you…!"

He put a hand over her mouth. "China!" he whispered. "Keep it down, okay? You're going to wake…"

She bit his hand and he dropped it with an expletive. "I can't even seem to wake *you* up!"

He hauled her with him to the bed, dropped her into the middle of it and landed beside her, a hand over her mouth again before she could react.

"I'm sorry," he said. And when she opened her mouth, intending to bite him again, he added, "and if you clamp those pearly whites on me again, you will be, too. Listen, okay? Just listen."

She wanted to. His weight leaning over her was delicious and she certainly understood his attitude. But it had been so far from the happy acceptance she'd hoped for that she didn't know where she stood.

She remained still, hostility waning quickly.

"I just want you to be sure, that's all," he said gently, brushing the hair back from her forehead. "I knew you woke up frightened and disoriented and you have all these old childhood feelings of not belonging and…I didn't want our making love to be any part of that."

"It isn't," she said firmly. "I did wake up frightened. In the dream I couldn't get out of the water because something was weighing me down. Then I woke up with you beside me and it was all so right and comfortable and I admitted to myself that I love you. And then the weight was gone. I understood why I dreamed that. I was drowning because I couldn't let myself feel the truth. And the moment I did, I felt like a Macy's balloon."

He blinked. "A what?"

"Lighter than air," she clarified. "Floating. And I thought you'd want to know that I love you."

"China!" He slipped an arm under her and pulled her over him as he lay back. "I'm very happy to know that. Honored. Awed. You know I love you."

"Yes."

"All right, then." He reached for the hem of her T-shirt and pulled it over her head. She helped him with his. They shucked panties and briefs and he wrapped her in his arms, taking a moment to simply enjoy being body to body with her, close enough to be uncertain whose heartbeat was whose.

She sighed against his throat, planted a kiss on his collarbone, and he was surprised to find himself enjoying the aesthetics of the moment. He'd always been a considerate but urgent lover, wanting to get to that place where there was no thought, only pleasure, wanting to take his partner there.

He wondered now why he'd always been in such a hurry. Maybe because he hadn't wanted to think then—about anything. He'd worked hard, loved well, lived for the day he could manage another estate and search out his strengths.

Right now, he didn't care about any of that. His area of concern right now was five feet six inches of beautiful woman.

He explored every inch of her, marveled at the flower-petal softness of flesh under his fingertips, the architectural brilliance of breast and hip, the warm, silken cavern that made her gasp and shudder when he touched her there.

CHINA MOVED her lips across Campbell's muscular shoulders, the jut of his ribs and his flat stomach, then lost track of her intentions when he hitched her leg over him and dipped a finger inside her.

She no longer felt like a Macy's balloon. She was still in flight, but she'd been inhabited by a frantic butterfly, velvet wings in rapid flutter. This could not be her body! In a matter of seconds it had reached a level of torturous anticipation she'd never experienced before.

"Campbell!" she gasped, surprised.

"Yes."

"I...need you!"

"That's why I'm here."

"No. I mean I…ah!…*need* you." She pulled on his shoulders to draw him to her, inside her.

"Bossy little devil," he teased, raising himself over her, entering her slowly, easing deeper until their connection was so complete she uttered a little groan. It became a cry of surprise as pleasure broke over her, pinned her to the pillows with exquisite power, held her there interminably, then finally set her free.

The butterfly fled, the balloon drifted to earth. She held on to Campbell's shoulders while her body settled, then she opened her eyes, expecting to see a different world. She felt so changed she was sure she'd left this room and been deposited somewhere else.

But it was his room. And there he was. Campbell rolled off her, pulled her into his shoulder and kissed her forehead. "You want to sleep?"

"No. Do you?"

"No. You thinking about breakfast?"

"No."

"Oh, I know. The bologna-and-pepper-jack sandwich. Grilled."

"No." She stretched against him, running her foot along his shin. "I was thinking about making love to you before breakfast."

He wound his fingers in her hair and gently raised her head so that he could look at her. "Didn't you just do that?"

"Yes. Marvelously. But you were particularly attentive to me and I was too lost in your…expertise to reciprocate."

"Believe me, it happened without your effort."

She pushed herself up so that she could plant a kiss

under his ribs. Then she smiled into his eyes. "Imagine what it will be like when I really try."

He pulled her over him and kissed her soundly. "I'm not sure I'd survive it."

She settled comfortably astride his hips and leaned down to kiss him again. "Shall we see?"

He made a small sound of pleasure when she touched him. "Let's."

He climaxed in a flatteringly brief amount of time. She had all kinds of ministrations planned, little tortures she thought might show him some small degree of what she felt. But she had time only to plant kisses down the middle of his body. When she began another upward sweep of them, he caught her waist, held her in place and brought her down on top of him.

She lay atop him in the warm aftermath and relished the touch of his artful hands possessively stroking the backs of her legs.

"You survived," she said lazily.

"I am heroic," he replied in the same tone.

She nipped at his shoulder. "Good. Now you can make me that bologna-and-pepper-jack sandwich."

CAMPBELL SAT across the table from China with the bright morning light pouring into the kitchen and wondered how he'd come this far without her. Making love to her had somehow altered his chemistry. He'd always been the cynic, the one impelled to protect himself and those he loved from every dangerous eventuality—even the emotional ones.

This morning, watching her polish off the begged-for

sandwich, he believed in every Pollyanna promise out there. All you need is love. Love conquers all. Love can change the world.

It had to be true. He was not the same man who'd gone to bed last night.

The first thing he'd done this morning as China showered was ride the perimeter of Shepherd's Knoll on the Vespa scooter to assure himself that the guards' shift change had been made without difficulty, and that everyone was alert.

But the need to protect his feelings and his fears seemed to have evaporated. He loved China, and there was no way he was leaving here without her. If they had to go to Canada first to straighten out her family story, that was fine, but she was going to Flamingo Gables with him.

She polished off the last bite of sandwich and smiled at him. Her eyes glowed with happiness, and he guessed his did, too. She wore a simple blue cotton shirt over her jeans today, and she'd caught her hair back in a fat, curly ponytail.

The sight of her filled him with both a raging lust and an almost disabling tenderness.

"Good job on the sandwich," she praised. "Did you like it?"

"I did," he admitted. "Though I'm not sure it beats the traditional bacon and eggs for breakfast or a good Denver omelet."

"The best thing about it—" she pushed away from the table, went to the freezer, and pulled out a carton of ice cream "—is that because it's a sandwich and not breakfast food, you can follow it with dessert." She opened the overhead cupboard in search of bowls. "Join me? It's coffee flavored."

He'd join her in the Sahara in August. And he was about to say so when the kitchen door burst open and Winfield stood there, his usually unflappable demeanor clearly flapped.

Campbell got to his feet, all kinds of ugly possibilities coming to mind. They'd caught an intruder. Someone had been hurt. Something had happened to Killian or Sawyer or his mother.

"What is it?"

Winfield tried to answer and settled for a shake of his head, instead. "You'd better come."

Campbell raced out the door after Winfield, aware that China followed. Halfway up the driveway that led to the road, two of the guards, guns drawn, had stopped a taxi, and the very upset driver was out of the cab and talking loudly and rapidly in heavily accented English.

"No trouble!" Those two words emerged clearly from the emotional spate of unidentifiable speech. "No terrorist!"

As Campbell approached, the cabbie seemed to understand that he was in charge and appealed to him, grabbing his shirtfront in both hands.

Winfield moved to intervene, but Campbell held him off, feeling fairly sure that anyone intending harm would have to be far less hysterical to get the job done.

"It's all right," Campbell said slowly. He could feel the man trembling. "Tell me what you're doing here."

"Now why does a cab go anywhere?" said a pretty

young woman he hadn't noticed before, as she climbed out of the cab. She had short dark hair, dark brown eyes and an attitude that reminded him sharply of…someone. She wore a silky white shirt over khaki shorts and had an air of confidence he had to admire. "To deliver a passenger, of course. What's the matter with all of you, anyway?"

Before he could try to explain, China ran around him and toward the young woman, shouting, "Janet!"

"China!" The young woman opened her arms and the two collided in a happy embrace.

For a moment, Campbell couldn't move or speak.

"I'm sorry," Winfield said in his ear. "I didn't know… I mean…I suspected maybe…is it…her? Can you tell?"

Campbell could. Looking at her was like being struck by lightning. Not that her features clearly said Abby— she'd been only fourteen months old the last time he'd seen her. But their connection had been as children, before all the screens and shields of adulthood protected one from contact on an elemental level. He shared her essence, her blood, the composition of her cellular structure.

If he felt changed this morning after making love with China, now he felt as though God had reached down and patted his head, saying, *There's more, Campbell. This is your sister.*

Life was no longer recognizable. Campbell wanted to speak, but he seemed to have no air in his lungs.

China drew her sister—*his* sister—toward him, probably reading in his eyes the inexplicable recognition. She put a hand on his arm in comfort, tears filling her eyes.

"Campbell, this is my sister, Janet Grant. Janet, my… my host, Campbell Abbott."

He noted Janet's quick glance at China at the hesitation, then her conclusion that he was somehow responsible for that. She offered her hand, studying his face for one prolonged moment. He watched her interested expression morph into something more complex, more questioning. She must have seen something she didn't understand.

And that was no surprise. He himself didn't understand anything anymore.

The child he remembered had grown into a beautiful young woman, surprisingly similar in coloring and height to China, though they shared no blood connection. He wanted to wrap her in his arms and tell her how much they'd missed her and worried about her and prayed for her. But he had to remember that she had no clue yet what was going on. So he shook her hand and welcomed her to Shepherd's Knoll.

Then, as Winfield retrieved Janet's bags from the trunk, Campbell gave the driver a large bill and apologized profusely for frightening him. The cabbie may not have understood the apology, but his eyes brightened at the bill and he bestowed a wide smile on everyone as he climbed back into the cab.

Campbell thanked the guards for their vigilance, introduced Janet as China's guest, then taking one of the two bags Winfield carried, followed China as she led her sister to the house.

He realized that he'd never answered Winfield's

question about Janet. "Yes," he said as Winfield trudged beside him up the driveway. "Abby's come home."

Kezia and Daniel greeted them on the porch. Campbell saw their avid search of her face for a clue to the child they remembered, then, probably unable to decide if she was Abby or not, they looked at him.

He nodded briefly, then introduced her as China's sister, Janet. He saw them try to withhold emotion, but Kezia failed miserably, bursting into tears.

Janet patted the woman's shoulder worriedly as she wept and frowned at China. "Did China tell you I'm demanding?" Janet teased. "Because it isn't true. She's always lied about me because it makes her look better. Has she invaded your kitchen yet to make her famous bologna-and-pepper-jack sandwiches? Well, please don't worry. I'm not at all like that."

"I'm sorry." Kezia dabbed at her eyes and fibbed, "It's just that she's so looked forward to your visit."

China hugged her. "Can she have the room next to mine? Sawyer never uses it anymore."

"Yes. I'll bring up some towels."

Campbell wasn't sure if Janet bought Kezia's excuse or not. Daniel sent him an apologetic look as he led Kezia off to the kitchen. Campbell took the second bag from Winfield and followed the women upstairs.

"I'm so happy to see you!" China said as she led Janet into the mostly white room. "Did you try to call me?"

Janet dropped a big purse on the colorful quilt that adorned the bed and leaned against a tall foot post. "I didn't get your message until the day before yesterday.

I'd gone to Jasper's Camp looking for my family. There are few refinements there, and definitely *no* cell phone towers. Then, when I got back and got word that you'd called, I was feeling grim and complicated emotions I just couldn't share over the phone. Then, my flights were scheduled so tightly I just ran from plane to plane. I intended to call you when I landed in New York, but there was an unclaimed taxi and I grabbed it. I've been so eager to see you." Those words were spoken with an air of sadness and disillusionment, then she looked around with a small smile and said, "What a lovely room. You're sure I'm not displacing anyone?"

"No," China assured her. "Most of the family's off doing other things for a few days. And this is a guest room, anyway."

Janet went to the window that looked out onto the backyard and part of the orchard. "It's beautiful here. Jasper's Camp was beautiful, too, but very remote. It had a tiny schoolhouse where all the grades were together in one classroom like those old frontier schools." She tossed her head, clearly trying to shake off the mood. She smiled at Campbell as he carried her bags to the wardrobe. "You're sure you don't mind my invading your home?"

"You're not invading," he replied, storing the bags in the bottom. "We're happy to have you."

"That's very generous of you." She caught China's hands and asked eagerly, "So…this is your family? Campbell is your brother?" She looked from China to Campbell, waiting for an explanation.

When she saw them exchange a look, she frowned worriedly. "What? This isn't your home?"

China put an arm around Janet's shoulders and squeezed. "How about a cup of tea? You must be tired after—"

"China, what is it? Don't try to put me off—just tell me. I hurried here when I got your message, hoping that your past was turning out better than mine and anxious to share that with you." She caught the hand around her shoulder. "If something's wrong, tell me. We decided we'll always have each other, remember?"

China bit her lip, holding back what looked like a need to cry. Campbell felt her pain, as well as real gratitude that she was not his sister.

"Okay," she said on an indrawn breath. "This is not my family. Campbell isn't my brother. But we think he might be yours."

Janet's eyes widened and her mouth fell open. She tried several times to speak but didn't seem to know what to say. She finally cleared her throat and said, "I think a cup of tea would be good."

Chapter Eleven

"My DNA test," China said, pouring boiling water over tea bags in a fat, brown pot on the kitchen table, "proved that I'm not an Abbott."

Janet was seated opposite Campbell. "Am I correct in assuming that you're happy about that?" she asked him.

"I am." He made no effort to explain or qualify his reply.

Janet smiled knowingly. "So that's how it is."

"Yes."

"Okay." She folded her arms, looking puzzled. "But I don't understand why the fact that China *isn't* an Abbott suggests to you that I *am*."

China left the tea to steep, then went looking for something to serve with it.

"There are apricot stars in the doughnut box," Campbell said. "Winfield and Daniel went to get doughnuts for the guys this morning, and I asked them to bring back some stars for you."

She was touched that he'd thought of doing that. She placed two apricot stars and the apple fritter she knew he preferred on a plate and put it beside the pot.

"Because it's the only explanation for why the box with my name was filled with all that stuff about Abigail Abbott's kidnapping," she explained. "Campbell's theory is that the lids with our names on them got switched at some point, maybe in one of our moves."

Janet was pensive for a moment, then looked around herself at the big kitchen, then beyond the windows to the large expanse of land, then back at China. "Wow," she said simply.

"Yeah." China brought three Abbott Mills mugs and sat down at the table.

"So how do we find out for sure?"

"You take the same DNA test," Campbell said, "and the lab compares it to Mom's."

Janet nodded, pulling an empty mug toward her and examining the logo. She glanced up at Campbell. "How old were you when Abigail was taken?"

"Five and half."

"Do you think I'm her?"

He nodded, a sweetly affectionate smile on his lips China had never seen there before. It spoke of fondness, of something shared that an outsider couldn't know. "I do."

"Do I look familiar?"

"No. But I felt something…I don't know…can't explain it…the moment I saw you. You and I are the only two siblings from our father's second wife. When you started to crawl, then toddle around, you made my life a misery. You were always in my toys, always grabbing things that were mine and, however unwittingly, destroying them."

She folded her arms on the table, smiling at his reminiscences. "If you don't mind, I'll withhold an apology until we know for sure that I'm to blame."

China poured a few drops of tea into her cup and, deciding it was well steeped, poured tea all around. As she worked, Campbell began to tell Janet about the Abbotts, about his brothers and Chloe. When she asked who kidnapped her, he explained that they'd never learned.

"The conclusion was that someone had gotten out with you through a basement window, because one of the windows that's always locked was unlocked, and there were boxes pushed up to it. But everyone who worked here then works here today, except the nanny, who was so crushed she eventually quit. And she'd been very good to all of us."

Campbell retrieved a photo from a shelf in the living room. It was one China had often admired. The photo that had been taken for the Abbotts' Christmas cards the year after Abby was born—Chloe and Nathan seated on a padded bench with the two older boys behind them, Campbell at his father's side, and Abby in her arms. They all wore red shirts for the photo, and the baby wore a red Santa hat. They looked so happy and so…unified. China felt a pang of jealousy.

Janet looked from the photo to Campbell. "I see you in the boy's face. Sweet but a little defensive."

He blinked at China. "Does that describe me?"

"To a *T*," she answered. She refocused on Janet. "We've all been waiting for you to return my call since the day we found out my DNA didn't match Chloe's. Killian had to go to the Abbott Mills office in London to take care of some problem. His wife is pregnant with twins, so he took her along. And Sawyer and his fiancée and her three children drove to Vermont to meet her family. Chloe was having fits waiting for you, and the doctor thought it would be good for her to have something else to think about while waiting for word from you. So Sawyer and Sophie took her and Tante Bijou with them."

"Tante who?"

"Bijou. A wonderful little old lady who practically raised Chloe. She's just recovering from complications of the flu. She lives in Paris, but she's been visiting here for a while."

"Are you up to meeting all those people?" Campbell asked.

Janet's eyes filled with tears and China reached over the table to catch her hand. "It's a lot to absorb, isn't it?"

Janet nodded, then put her other hand over China's. "It is, but I was thinking that…if the box lids were mixed up and I am…oh, God!…if I am Abigail Abbott, then you're…"

China nodded, unwilling to let her sister feel any guilt or remorse that their positions were reversed. "I'm the contents of your box. And that's okay. We both set off on our searches to learn the truth, and I don't want someone else's. I want mine."

"But…it's…I mean, it isn't…"

"Just tell me."

"Okay." Janet sat up a little straighter and tightened her grip on China's hand. "I finally tracked down my…or I guess, maybe, your godmother from the sig-

nature on the bottom of the birth certificate. She was in
a nursing home and sort of in and out of dementia. But
she perked up when I said the name Margaret Roberts—the mother's name on the birth certificate. She
said they were good friends as girls. But—" Janet hesitated and squared her shoulders "—Margaret died with
her parents in an automobile accident in 1980."

China withheld a reaction despite the deep hole that
opened up right in the center of her being. Janet's hand
tightened on hers. "I asked her about the baby's father,
but she didn't seem to be able to process the thought.
Or maybe she just couldn't remember."

Janet pulled a silver chain out from inside her shirt.
On it was strung a gold ring with a heart-shaped garnet
stone. She pulled it off and tried to give it to China.
"This was hers, I think. It was in the bottom of the box.
I guess it's yours now."

China pushed her hand back. "You keep it until we
get the results of the DNA test." She wasn't sure why
she did that. Perhaps because she didn't want to own her
place in that tragic story. Campbell was sure he recognized Janet, so she must be Abigail, which probably
meant that China was Margaret Roberts's daughter.

She didn't realize until that moment what a tragedy it
was to never be able to set eyes on the woman who bore
you. Oh, she'd loved Bob and Peggy Grant, appreciated
the wonderful parents they'd been, and the need to lay
eyes on Margaret in no way diminished the love she felt
for them. It was just…oh, blood calling to blood—the
same thing that made Campbell recognize Janet.

"China, please take it." Janet held it out again.

China shook her head, knowing her sister felt guilty that she was probably going to belong to this Abbott life, and she wanted China to have *some*thing. But China truly didn't want it.

Campbell held his hand out and Janet unfastened the chain and dropped the ring into his palm.

"I'll hold it until we're sure whose it is," he said. "Janet, I promised to call my family the minute we heard you were coming."

Janet nodded. "Yes, do. Tell them I'm…I'm anxious to meet them, whatever the results."

"I'm sure they feel the same. Can I steal China from you for a minute? Then you can have time to rest or tour the place or whatever you'd like to do."

"Yes. I'll have another cup of tea."

Campbell caught China's hand and took her with him onto the porch that looked out on the orchard. The day was brilliant and warm, the scene bucolic and beautiful, nature apparently unaware that Margaret Roberts had died far too young and left a baby who would never know her.

Emotions churned inside China—joy that Janet might be part of this family she'd come to love so much, loss and a very pointed sadness that her own mother was beyond her reach.

She forced a smile for Campbell. "Don't you love her? I can't wait to know for sure that she's your sister. Are you going to call Chloe right away?"

Something had happened to China with the arrival of her sister. She'd been thrilled to see her, seemed genuinely happy that she was probably an Abbott.

Campbell thought he understood China's feelings of being adrift in a world without family, even while he wished she was more pleased with the fact that it left her free to marry him.

Marry him. It jarred him a little to think of their relationship in those terms. Up to this moment, he'd simply thought of her in his bed, going to Florida with him, part of his life.

Marry him. That shook him for a moment, then seemed to settle inside him—another truth dealt with. Now. What to do about that lost look in her eyes.

He sat on the porch railing, his back resting against a pillar, and drew her close so that they were eye-to-eye. "I'm sorry your mother's gone," he said.

He saw the pain in her gaze, though she simply hitched a shoulder as though to tell him she could cope. "Oh, that's the breaks, I guess. You can't take a complex situation like this and think there's going to be a happy ending for everyone."

She stood stiffly in his arms. He guessed she wanted out of this conversation. She'd arrived here insisting she didn't want anything from anyone except to learn her parentage, and now that she had, she didn't want anyone feeling sorry for her.

"We're going to have a happy ending," he insisted.

"The Abbotts?" She smiled again. "Yes, you will. Janet's a wonderful—"

"I'm talking about you and me," he said. "We're going to get married and live happily ever after."

Her eyes met his, and the look in them hit him like a fist in the face. She tried to cover the firm *No, we're not* in them with a frowning, thoughtful look, but he saw it, anyway. "Campbell, that's a little bit of a leap."

He tightened his grip on her even as she put her hands on his arms, preparing to push her way out of them. "Why would you say that? We just made love like two people who've been waiting a lifetime for each other."

She looked into his eyes again, and this time they were filled with the love he knew she felt for him. But under it all, that negative claim remained. "It was…beyond anything I'd imagined. But now…everything's different."

"Like what?"

"Like everything," she said, her voice thick with emotion. "Abby's back. You *knew* her. The whole family dynamic will change. You'll all have to adjust. You should take time to get acquainted, to help her become part of the family. You're the very one who should do that for her because you're the one who understands her best. You're the two with everything in common."

"Why does that mean you can't stay?"

"Because I don't belong."

"That isn't true, but if you think you don't because you're not an Abbott, that'll change if you marry me."

"But everyone will think I'm doing it because it's the only way I can be part of the family."

He rolled his eyes in exasperation. "That isn't true, either! Everyone wants you to stay."

And then she said the only thing that could give him pause. "*I'm* not sure it wouldn't be true."

She looked ashamed at her alarming honesty. She pushed against him a little harder, but he continued to hold on. "You want to get away," he said baldly, suddenly realizing how desperate she was to escape if she could even think that, how little he understood her and how much that hurt. "Even though this is resolving itself in the best way possible, you want to run."

"I want to give her space."

"You want to run and cause yourself pain because you didn't find the storybook beginning you'd hoped for. And you're willing to throw away the life you could make for yourself as an adult, because you can't find a connection to your childhood."

Her expression hardened. "Isn't that why you're running away?" she challenged. "You have to work somewhere else even though life is ideal here and everyone loves you here, because your brothers are too perfect and you don't want to have to be held to that standard? You keep saying that you can't find yourself in their shadow, but I think you just don't want to have to live up to them. You *have* the connection I can't find, but you don't appreciate it. So I don't think you can judge me."

Campbell couldn't believe that he'd brought her out here on the porch to offer comfort, and that the situation had turned into this hurtful encounter. He dropped his hands from her, deciding it was time to stop.

"Very well, then." He stood and she took a step back, looking a little regretful. "You do what you have to do, and I'll do what works for me. Maybe one day our paths will cross again. Or maybe not. The notion that we should get married was probably a leap, after all. Excuse me. I have some phone calls to make. Why don't you show Janet around?"

He left her standing there, looking like a poster child for heartbreak and regret, went into his office and closed the door.

He spoke to Sawyer first, thinking it might be best if Sawyer broke the news to their mother. As they spoke on his brother's cell phone, Campbell could hear the children in the background and Tante Bijou exclaiming in French. There was high, feminine laughter.

"Do you think…she's Abby?" Sawyer asked in a voice just above a whisper.

"Yes, I do," Campbell replied. "I can't tell by her looks, of course, although she reminds me a lot of Mom. But I just…felt something when I first saw her. I don't think it's a mind-over-matter thing. But when you all get back here, we'll find out for sure."

"Okay. We're having a good time with Sophie's relatives, but I don't imagine they'll mind if we cut short this invasion by a couple of days. I'll tell Mom right away, and I'm thinking she'll want to go home immediately. In which case, we'll see you tonight."

"Good. I'll let Kezia know." Campbell dialed Killian, who picked up on the third ring, speaking quietly.

"Can you talk?" Campbell asked.

"I'm in a meeting. Is it important?"

"Yeah."

There was a moment's heavy silence. "Abby?"

"Yeah."

"Hold on."

Campbell heard Killian excuse himself from the meeting, heard footsteps, a door opening and closing.

"Okay," Killian said finally. "I'm in a stairwell."

"Janet's here. She just showed up, rather than calling first."

"Ah. Impetuous. An Abbott trait, at least in the younger children."

"Ha-ha. How's Cordie doing? Can you come home?"

"She's great. My meeting's just wrapping up—all ruffled feathers smoothed and an increase in our fall order. Cordie and I'll take an early-morning flight out of Heathrow. You okay?"

"Yeah."

"You sound…not okay. You don't like her?"

"No, she seems great. Just like we'd want her to be. It's China and—" he sighed "—it's a long story."

"Okay. You can tell me about it when I get home."

"Or not."

"Come on. You know I thrive on setting your life to rights."

"Heaven help me. Call me with the flight number so I can tell Daniel."

"Right. See you in the morning.

Campbell hung up and went looking for Brian. He was nowhere to be found.

"He and Winfield went to his shop," Daniel told him when he sought him out in the garage. He pointed to the overturned square-stern canoe in the only empty spot. It looked sound, but desperately needed a paint job. "Brought it back to work on, so he'd have something to do while waiting for the delivery of his goods."

"Where is he now?"

"Not certain. He helped Winfield carry doughnuts out to the guys. He might still be there somewhere, on the line."

"Thanks, Daniel."

"Sure. Something wrong, Mr. Campbell?" Daniel gave him a probing look, and Campbell knew he could share his troubles or not, as he wished. Kezia would have shaken it out of him.

Appreciating Daniel's easy manner, Campbell clapped him on the shoulder. "Nothing I can't fix," he replied. "Thanks."

"Sure."

Campbell walked through the vintage orchard. The thinning was finished, and the small, hard fruit was developing nicely.

He remembered China working hard on the Duchess and thought he was right about why she was suddenly so anxious to put distance between herself and him. Was it only last night that they were so close it would have been hard to tell whose limbs were whose?

He refused to consider that he wouldn't be able to change her mind. He figured she was making decisions based partially on an altruistic wish to stay out of her sister's life, and a real desire not to have to watch her sister live the life she'd thought was hers.

He wouldn't believe that she didn't love him, that her lovemaking could have had everything to do with her desire to be part of his family, not life with him.

Suddenly weary, he sat under the Duchess, hoping for inspiration. If China's natural mother were still alive, he felt fairly sure this would have all gone differently. Good or bad, the woman would have given her the connection she seemed to need so much. China would have had facts, details, and she'd have been able to figure out how she'd come to be and then move on.

Now, all she had was a dead woman's name on a birth certificate and no idea who her father was.

Campbell took the birthstone ring out of his pocket and studied it. It was a pretty stone with nice color, but probably of no great value, except that the heart shape suggested there might be sentiment attached to it.

The ring was small, fit only to the first knuckle on his little finger. So Margaret Roberts had probably been slender, maybe even petite. He wondered if her parents had given it to her.

He studied the ring closely, looking for an inscription or something that would give him a clue to Margaret Roberts' personality. Then an odd mechanical sound, a man's shout and a high-pitched feminine scream caused him to start and almost drop the ring in the grass. He replaced it quickly in his shirt pocket and sprang to his feet, looking for the source of trouble. There was another scream and more shouting, coming from the direction of the driveway.

Daniel came out of the garage to listen, then followed Campbell as he hurried to the head of the driveway. Once there, Campbell saw the upended Vespa, and the three bodies lying in the middle of the lane. Oh, God. He'd told China to show Janet around. He headed off at a run, Daniel right behind him.

Bodies were stirring as he approached. China and Janet were helping each other up, and Brian lay on his back, propped up on his elbows, looking around him as though unable to figure out what had happened. Campbell went to the women and Daniel to Brian.

"Are you all right?" he asked, helping China haul Janet to her feet. Both women were covered in dust kicked up by the bike. Instinctively he put his handkerchief to a scrape on China's cheek, then turned to Janet. She looked sound if a little disheveled, and in her eyes flashed fire, an Abbott trait if there ever was one.

"Didn't your mother teach you," she demanded of Brian, who stood across the lane, brushing himself off, "never to jump out into the road from behind a parked car?"

Brian made a production of looking up and down the lane. "Do you see a parked car?"

"Parked trees, then," she amended. "Same thing. You know what I mean. Stepping out into the road like that from a place where no one can see you is dangerous."

"I'm sure walking anywhere near where you're driving would be dangerous," he countered. "Even the sidewalk."

"Brian," Campbell interrupted quickly, stepping between them in an attempt to defuse the argument. "This is China's adopted sister, Janet Grant. I think she's…our sister."

Janet stared at him a moment, her brow furrowing. "*Our* sister? Yours and…*his?*"

Campbell nodded. "Yes. It's a little complicated. Our father's first wife had a fling with our neighbor, and Brian is the result of that liaison. No blood relation to you and me, but that doesn't count for anything in this house." He gave China a quick, significant glance at that, then turned his attention back to Janet. "Janet, I'd like you to meet Brian Girard."

Brian took several steps toward her and extended his hand. "Pleased to meet you. Pardon the tire track up my face."

Janet smiled sweetly. "That's all right. Men who leap out from behind poplar trees, driving unsuspecting women off the road, should wear an identifying mark."

"Janet," China chided gently, "Brian's a great guy. I'm sure he didn't mean to cause an accident. And you have to remember that the Vespa isn't Jerry Watson's Harley." China explained in an aside, "She once wiped out an art show on La Cienega Boulevard learning to ride her boyfriend's bike."

Janet frowned at her in annoyance, her mouth open to reply, then she expelled a breath and changed her mind. "I'm sorry," she said to Brian. "I was going a little fast."

"You were airborne." Brian delivered that implacable assessment as he righted the bike. He pointed to the incline in the direction of the house that might have caused the mishap. Then he straddled the bike. "Get on and I'll show you how to handle it without killing anyone."

Campbell caught China's and Daniel's surprised glances as he tried to figure out how this was going to play out. Had Campbell and China been enacting this little scene, she'd have stormed away and let him ride back to the house by himself.

Janet, it seemed, had ideas of her own on how to deal with Brian. She climbed on behind him. "Remember, please, that I might be your long-lost sister, and you wouldn't want to get rid of me before my mother's seen me."

"I might be doing her a favor," Brian said, then

revved the motor and said, "Hold on!" as the bike shot away. They disappeared over the rim of the hill.

Daniel grinned at Campbell. "That's interesting," he said.

"She *was* going a little fast." China picked up a scarf Campbell didn't recognize and stuffed it into her pocket. "But she drives to work on a bike, so I wasn't worried. We did take the hill at a good rate of speed, but she was in control until Brian walked out of the woods and messed up her concentration."

"Technically," he countered as they began to walk back toward the house, "you're not in control if someone can mess up your concentration."

"You're sounding like a big brother already." She stopped to flex her knee. "Reminds me of the way you treated me my first couple of weeks here. Ow."

"Scraped knee?" he asked, bending down to look at it. She'd worn long pants today, fortunately, instead of her usual shorts. They were too snug to pull up, but there was a tear and blood on the knee.

"Yeah. Just stings a little."

"Want me to carry you?"

"No." She even took a step back. "I'm fine. It just stings a little."

He put his hands in his pockets. "Then put your arm in mine and you can lean on me," he said.

She did. Daniel had kept walking once he'd concluded she wasn't hurt, figuring, Campbell guessed, that they might appreciate privacy.

"Thank you," she said grudgingly. "I thought you weren't speaking to me."

"I'm not. I'm just providing support."

"Is everybody coming home?"

"Yes. Sawyer expects to be home tonight. Killian and Cordie are taking an early-morning flight out of Heathrow. With the time difference they'll be home in the morning."

They trudged on silently for a while, then as they reached the house, she asked seriously, "Are you okay? Is she everything you hoped for, or is it hard to even feel anything after all this time?"

"No, I'm not okay," he replied candidly. "But we can't blame that on Abby…Janet. I hardly know her, yet she seems very familiar to me. I think we have a connection that transcends the time apart."

She nodded. Apparently she wasn't going to ask him why he wasn't okay.

He helped her up the steps and into the library.

"Excuse me," she said. "I'll go change my clothes and put something on my knee."

"You need help up the stairs?"

"No, I can manage. Thanks. Where are they, anyway?"

"Who?"

"Brian and Janet?"

"Maybe on a tour of the place."

She frowned at Campbell from the fourth stair up. "I didn't think they liked each other."

"You didn't like me," he reminded her, "yet you made love to me most of last night."

She pursed her lips impatiently. "Hardly the same thing."

"That," he said, "remains to be seen."

Chapter Twelve

Campbell expected a commotion like Christmas when his family came home. He imagined everyone storming through the doors, all talking at once, probably scaring Janet out of her wits.

But a certain solemnity seemed to have taken over the moment. Janet didn't want to go to bed, so they'd all sat up, playing Trivial Pursuit at the dining-room table.

Kezia insisted on staying up to provide them with coffee and snacks, and certain that the family would need something to eat when they arrived. Daniel helped her prepare.

Campbell and Brian tried to keep the mood light, but as the evening wore on, the tension tightened until Janet, who'd been murdering all of them with her knowledge of Hollywood trivia, couldn't remember who'd starred in *The Flying Nun*. She finally pushed away from the table.

"Sally Field would be upset with you," China teased.

Then a guard called to tell Campbell that Sawyer had just passed his checkpoint and was headed for the house.

In a moment they heard a car coming up the driveway. It was almost midnight. Janet turned to China in panic.

"No need to be afraid." China put an arm around her shoulders and squeezed. "They're the nicest people in the world. I hope with all my heart that you're Abby. You're going to love them."

Janet drew back to look at her, her eyes brimming with tears. "I'm sorry you're not. You love them, too." She hugged her. "Of course, that allows you and Campbell to…"

That sentence remained unfinished as they heard Winfield's footsteps on the front stoop and heard the door open. They heard Chloe's greeting to him, then her footsteps coming in the direction of the living room, where they all stood.

China grabbed Janet's hand and drew her to the middle of the room. Chloe appeared in the doorway and stopped, pulling a silky scarf from around her neck. She wore a pale green skirt and sweater, and she looked both energized and exhausted. Her eyes quickly went over China with a smile, then stopped on Janet. Her gaze roved Janet's face feature by feature, then tears filled Chloe's eyes and she tipped her head in a gesture that told Campbell she felt precisely as he had when he'd first seen Janet. She recognized Abby.

Tears streamed down Janet's face as China, crying too, pushed her gently toward Chloe. Chloe opened her arms and Janet went into them.

Campbell wrapped his arms around China.

After a moment Sawyer appeared behind Chloe, with Sophie and the children standing back. Chloe straightened to draw him close and said in a strangled voice, "Abby, this is your brother, Sawyer."

Sawyer looked Janet over, the line of his mouth firmed, then he took her in his arms and wept. Brian turned away, a hand to his face, and Campbell cleared his throat to try to keep the tears at bay.

He thought he'd managed until China turned to him, clearly intending to offer the comfort he'd offered her. And then…he lost it.

After all this time, after all the anguish, the guilt, the special family days that were never quite perfect because someone was missing, Abby was home. He thought about his father, who'd died with Abby's name on his lips and hoped he was watching. His mother would finally have her daughter for girl talk and shopping trips, and his brothers would finally be free of the guilt of having failed their little sister.

And then there was him. Janet…Abby…seemed so sane a young woman, so well-adjusted to her life even with that early major upheaval, that certainly she could forgive the brother who'd yanked his toy truck away from her and bruised her tiny little arm.

While he felt that large hole in his life mend itself, he couldn't help but worry about the woman who held him in comfort, her cheek pressed into his shoulder. He appreciated her willingness to share his emotion when *her* feelings had to be in terrible turmoil.

His mother reached an arm out for him, and he joined her and Sawyer and Janet in a shared embrace. Chloe sobbed uncontrollably.

When she composed herself again, she reached for

Brian, who tried to resist until Janet told Chloe, "He doesn't like me, because I ran him down with the Vespa. He doesn't want to be my brother."

Brian joined their circle with a wry glance at Chloe. "I think the first thing you should do as her mother is take away the keys."

Sawyer brought Sophie and the children into the circle and introduced them to Janet.

Campbell saw China try to slip away, but caught her by the back of her shirt and drew her in, despite her resistance.

"When China and I started this search for our parents," Janet said, pulling China in beside her, "we promised each other that whatever happened, we would always be sisters. So she has to be your daughter and your sister, too." She spoke firmly as her gaze covered Chloe, Sawyer, Brian and him.

"Of course," his mother said, "we've all made it clear she is adopted."

Sawyer nodded. "Absolutely."

"Yes," Brian agreed.

"No," Campbell said. When everyone looked at him in confused surprise, he added, "I have other plans for her."

"Ah," his mother said with a happy expression. *"L'amour."*

China gave him a scolding look that he ignored.

"I'm hungry," Eddie complained to Janet.

"Well, I am, too." Janet took his hand, reached for Emma with the other. "I was so nervous about meeting all of you that I couldn't eat dinner." She smiled at Gracie. "Let's go see what Kezia's cooking up."

Gracie, who'd grown close to China while her mother visited Sawyer and Shepherd's Knoll, caught her arm. "Want to come, too? I have to show you the cool sweatshirt I bought in Vermont."

Campbell, Brian, Sawyer, Cordie and Chloe all watched China and Janet and the children walk away. Campbell understood their fascination. It was a little slice of what they'd always dreamed of and feared would never come true. Janet…Abby…as an adult in her home, being a part of their lives, an aunt to Sawyer's children.

Sawyer put a hand to his chest, his voice still heavy with emotion. "I *knew* her."

Chloe, both hands over her heart, nodded as fresh tears fell. "I did, too. She is Abby. I can't wait for Killian to see her."

As Chloe joined the women and children in the kitchen, Sawyer held Campbell and Brian back. "Winfield told me a little about what's going on," he said, "but I want details. And why didn't you call me?"

"Because I have it under control," Campbell replied, leading the way to the library, "and I wanted you to enjoy your visit. Come on. I'll tell you the whole story."

DANIEL LEFT the house at six the following morning to meet Killian and Cordie's flight, which was due to arrive at seven-thirty. Kezia packed coffee, scones and fruit, certain they would need food.

Sawyer called the hospital to set up the DNA test and was told the hospital would expect them anytime that day.

China sat on the bed in Janet's room while Janet got

ready. Her sister looked worried, China thought, as she wandered in and out of the bathroom.

"Can't find my blow-dryer," Janet said. "I'm sure I brought it." She looked in the bottom of her wardrobe. "I was sure I'd put it away."

"Want to borrow mine?"

"No, thanks. It has to be here someplace." Janet checked the shelf in the closet, the dresser drawers in which she'd put lingerie and tops, then disappeared into the bathroom again. China followed her to the doorway and spotted the dryer on a small shelf built into an organizer above the tub.

"There," she said, pointing to the large, lavender appliance.

Janet rolled her eyes at its obviousness. "Thank you. I guess I'm a little shaken this morning." She plugged in the blow-dryer, then looked at China in the mirror, her eyes wide with distress. "It's all just beginning to dawn on me. I mean, look around! Could I really be part of this?"

China took a few steps closer until she was reflected over Janet's shoulder in the mirror. "Why not?"

"Well. All this style and obvious wealth. I'm just a simple, Southern California girl. If this is my life…do I really belong in it?"

"You encouraged me to check it out when we thought I might be Abby."

Janet turned around to face her, the blow-dryer still in her hand like a weapon with which she might do herself harm. "That's because you're so calm and contained. You can fit in anywhere and be welcome. You bring serenity to any situation."

"You're a stockbroker," China reminded her, completely surprised by her fears. "You're their kind of people."

Janet turned back to the mirror and studied her face with disappointment. "No, I'm not. I *work* for their kind of people, but I don't live among them. I'd be scared to death."

"Of what?"

Janet evaded an answer by turning on the blow-dryer and running it wildly over her short, wet hair. She ruffled it with her fingers, pulled at her bangs, then turned it off again with a reflected frown at China. "Did you see how much Chloe needs me to be Abby? The fact that I might be is as scary as the possibility that I might not. Her baby has been missing for twenty-five years. How could I possibly live up to what she imagines Abigail has become. I mean, given her breeding and all those Abbott qualities that should have flourished in her no matter where she was? Do you really see any of that in me?"

China moved closer to squeeze Janet's shoulders. "I see all of it. But I think the important thing to remember is that all you have to live up to is what you want for *yourself,* the goals you want to accomplish, the ways you want to excel. That's all they want of each other."

"What if I am Abby? What if I disappoint them?"

"I don't think that could happen."

Janet groaned and turned to hug her. "That's a very sisterly thing to say. I wonder how true it is."

"It's true. Despite the family's closeness, they really give each other a lot of scope. Campbell loves his brothers, but he's always felt as though he's in their shadow and wants to see what he can accomplish on his own. They don't want him to go, but they want him to do what he feels he has to to be happy."

Janet finished her hair with a few more roars of the blow-dryer, and a few rolls of a round brush. Her shiny dark hair settled into a cheek-hugging, fashionably mussy cap around her face.

She put the blow-dryer back on the shelf and opened her makeup bag on the white-tile counter. "You're in love with Campbell," she said matter-of-factly as she powdered her smooth complexion.

They'd never lied to each other. They'd *tricked* each other as children, but they'd never lied to each other.

"Yes."

"He's in love with you."

"Yes."

Janet applied a light blush. "Then, why don't you look happy?"

"I'm happy," China argued, trying to prove it with a forced smile. Janet gave her a look that said she didn't believe her. "All right," China said defensively. "It's been a pretty turbulent time. I mean, we thought I was Abby, and I had all the same fears you're experiencing, then I turned out not to be. Which was good, because by that time I knew I didn't *want* to be Campbell's sister."

"True, but the problem, as you see it, is that you still don't know who you are. Am I right?"

"Yes. And that's a whole new set of issues. I can love Campbell, but can I really if everybody in my past is dead and I have no real knowledge of who I am?"

Janet applied light strokes of mascara, then frowned at China. "Does that matter to Campbell?"

"He says no."

"Then…?"

China sank onto a small green padded bench that matched the trim on the towels. "I love this family. I'd have loved to be part of it." She added quickly, "And I in no way resent the fact that you are blood-related, instead. I think that's wonderful."

When Janet nodded her understanding, China went on. "How do I know that I'm not in love with him because it would let me into the family, after all?"

"Because you've never used anyone in your life for any reason."

"But we hated each other in the beginning." China explained about Chloe being in Paris and the family's decision to wait until she returned before doing a DNA test. "So Killian thought it would be good if I helped Campbell on the estate so that I'd get acquainted with it and him. He never did believe I was Abby, but that I was a gold digger. And I resented his cynical, despotic approach to running this place."

"Love's like that sometimes, isn't it?" Janet asked, applying a light lipstick, then tossing everything back into her bag. "You end up with the person who seemed least likely to make you happy. Happens with stocks on occasion. What's a real dog in the beginning can get an influx of new life, a change of management, of approach, of direction, and then suddenly you're making a bundle on it."

China sighed, took Janet's brush, and ran it through her own hair. Her sister looked fresh and bright, despite her concerns. She'd tried to perk up her own look this morning by piling her hair up and wearing a flowered pink shirt that put color in her cheeks. She didn't want to do anything to rain on Janet's parade.

"I think, Janet, we need some time apart to figure out what we really want. When I came here, Campbell had accepted a job managing an estate in Florida and was all set to go until his mom had a sort of anxiety attack. Since both his brothers were taking off in different directions, he decided to stay just until you showed up."

"Me?"

"Yes. By then we knew I wasn't Abby, and Campbell developed this theory that Abby must be you. I left that message for you and we were all waiting for you to call back. The point I'm making is that he's wanted to work somewhere else most of his adult life, and though I think he's crazy, because Shepherd's Knoll is so great and he's happy here, I'd like him to have that chance, and he won't feel free if he's committed to me."

"What if he wants to be committed to you?"

"Then…I'd have to save him from himself."

Janet opened her mouth to reply to that when they heard the slamming of the limousine doors and Chloe's excited shout of "Abby!" corrected quickly by "Janet! Killian's here!"

"Oh, my gosh." Janet shook her wrists nervously. "I heard about him in my class on management styles of CEOs. He's a genius."

"He's also the nicest man you'd ever want to meet."

"But…if he's my brother…"

"It seems he is."

"I don't think I have an Abbott brain."

"The family just wants you to have an Abbott *heart*. Lighten up. You're going to love him. And Cordie's a kick."

China had to literally drag Janet to the stairs. When Killian heard them coming, he strode into the hall from the living room to watch them descend.

Janet froze halfway down. Killian wore stone-colored slacks and a dark-blue knit shirt, but the casual attire did nothing to diminish the patriarchal air he wore, especially now that the family was expanding.

China saw his lips part slightly as he put a hand to the newel post—possibly to steady himself. In his case, too, recognition.

China tugged Janet to follow her to the bottom. When Janet stepped onto the carpet, Killian took her chin in his hand and studied her upturned face.

"My God!" he whispered. "It *is* you." Then he hugged her fiercely.

After a moment, the whole family crowded round. Killian introduced Cordie, who had to wipe away tears.

Kezia served coffee on a cart in the living room, the big room allowing everyone to feel comfortable. China stayed for a few minutes, long enough to check on Cordie's health and that of the babies, to tease Sophie's children, to allow Chloe to hug her and Brian to tease her.

Hoping she could escape Campbell without having to explain why she was leaving, she noted that he and Sawyer stood across the room in deep conversation.

She took advantage of the moment and slipped out. She ran to the orchard, not at all unhappy that Janet was so accepted, but just needing a moment away from the all-encompassing Abbotts. She wasn't one of them, and the sooner she got away, the better it would be for all concerned and the easier it would be for Janet to settle in.

She stood under the Duchess, noting that its fruit was growing though still green. Campbell said they would harvest in mid- to late September. It hurt to think she'd be gone by then.

In spite of the knowledge that she would be able finally to assume her own life, she felt a terrible sadness.

She stared at the house, hoping Sawyer would come out looking for her. Or come out to walk the orchard as he did almost every day, keeping a close eye on the condition of the fruit.

But this was no ordinary day. Abby was home. Somewhat lost to China, but home.

CAMPBELL SAW China slip away, but he didn't follow. He wanted to; he knew she was feeling out of place and probably a little as though she'd lost her sister to the Abbotts. It was a self-imposed pain, he thought, but he hated to think she was in pain for whatever reason.

Still, he had a better way to serve her today than to run after her and reassure her that she was loved and wanted.

Besides, he had a lot of explaining to do to Killian about the reason for the tight security and why he hadn't called to tell Killian about the fire. He was surprised when Sawyer came to his defense with a firmly spoken "Because we left him in charge, and he's taking care of it."

The moment Campbell was able to escape his brothers, he went into his office and locked the door. He dug

Margaret Roberts' ring out of his pocket and held it under the work light on his desk. He'd thought he'd seen something on the inside of the band yesterday in the orchard, just before he'd heard the Vespa crash.

He studied it now and thought he'd been mistaken. And then he saw the almost faded inscription in the gold. The letters were so worn, he couldn't quite decipher them, and could see that Janet might have missed them.

He took a felt-tip marker from his pencil cup and ran it several times over the inscription. The engraving took the ink and he was able to make out, MR then a heart, then ZS. MR. Margaret Roberts? Loves ZS? ZS. China's father? All he had to do was find out who ZS was, even though the trail was twenty-five years old.

Hell. Abby was back. He found himself believing in miracles.

LIFE SOMEHOW WENT ON, despite the high level of emotion on all fronts. Chloe and Janet had the DNA test, and the whole family settled down to wait. Killian went back to work in the city, one of Winfield's men with him, and Sawyer took up the issues of the foundation while helping Sophie plan their wedding. He and Sophie and the children lived at her place, one of Winfield's men also in residence there to keep them safe, but Sawyer still used his office at Shepherd's Knoll, and they took many of their meals there.

The children spent their days on the estate and Daniel, always accompanied by one of Winfield's men, took them to their various lessons—ballet, karate, summer crafts, swimming—waited for them and brought them home.

Chloe went over the plans Karen Benning submitted for the addition, and approved them with enthusiasm. The work began immediately, and checking on the workers' progress was added to Campbell's daily list of things to do.

China spoke to Campbell politely, but prevented discussion of the little intimacies they'd once talked about so easily, and allowed no reference to the night they'd made love or his proposal of marriage. Consequently, he had very little to talk about. The weather was perpetually beautiful, and no one particularly cared about politics, considering all that was going on at Shepherd's Knoll.

The women spent most of their time preparing for a large party Chloe intended to throw when the test proved that Janet was Abby. The subject of her name itself became such an issue that Campbell finally dubbed her Janby, a combination of her two personas.

Cordie designed an invitation Killian had printed in town, and they all helped address them for mailing. They polished silver, polished woodwork, helped wash the old Limoges china, worked under Kezia's leadership to prepare the house for the several hundred guests.

They'd all been working so hard that when a courier arrived one afternoon with an envelope for Miss Janet Grant, everyone was surprised into remembering that so far, Janet's membership in the Abbott family was a supposition and not a scientific fact.

As China had done, Janet held the letter until everyone had gathered for dinner.

"Whatever the results," she said, looking around the table as she picked up a butter knife and prepared to

open the envelope, "I want you to know how much I've
enjoyed being here, how much I appreciate your hospitality, and how much fun it's been to be Janby."

Killian assumed his role as spokesperson. "And we
want you to know that we decided to adopt China when
she turned out not to be ours. You've been voted in, too.
Open it up."

China watched her sister's face, remembering how
she'd felt when she'd read her own report, how complicated her feelings had been, because she hadn't wanted
to lose the Abbotts but she'd already suspected she was
falling in love with Campbell.

Of course, Janet suffered from no such warring
emotions.

Her eyes filled, she put a shaky hand to her mouth,
and everyone around the table held a collective breath.

"It seems adoption won't be necessary," she said,
her voice also shaky. She handed the report to Chloe,
who sat beside her. "Apparently, I'm an Abbott."

The commotion was earsplitting. There was laughing, crying, shouts, cheers, and Kezia and Daniel came
out of the kitchen with champagne and apple cider and
a tray of glasses.

China's heart rose into her throat with happiness for
her sister, then something landed like lead in the pit of
her stomach because Janet was theirs now, no longer
hers. Oh, they'd made the promise and Janet would honor
it, not out of duty but because they had shared so much
and been there for each other throughout their lives.

But China knew Janet would be worried about it all
the time, wanting to make sure China felt welcome,

wanting to be certain her attentions were split between her new family—actually her *old* family—and her adopted sister.

Well. At least now China was free to go with the knowledge that Janet would be happy and safe, that all her questions about the past were answered, and she was back in the loving arms of the family who'd awaited her safe return for so long.

Dinner seemed to go on forever. Victory had given the family an appetite and there seemed to be no end of delectable accompaniments to the steak and shrimp dinner. China kept up her end of various conversations that seemed to take place across the table or from one end of the table to another. If these conversations could be charted, she guessed they would look like one of those airline destination maps that crisscrossed in complicated patterns from one coast to the other.

Chloe looked as though she'd had the world handed to her, the brothers were full of cheerful insults for each other and competed for Janet's attention. Cordie and Sophie talked about flowers for Sophie and Sawyer's wedding, and whether or not to have the reception at home.

Sophie and Sawyer's wedding! China had almost forgotten it was taking place on Labor Day. Even if she did escape the house, she'd have to be back for the wedding. She had the dress and the shoes and a very saucy little hat.

She had the most unsettling feeling that she would never be free of Shepherd's Knoll and the people in it. If she left, she suspected the time she'd spent here with them would live with her forever, the memories held up against every new experience to measure how it compared.

The party finally broke up about ten o'clock. Everyone wandered off to their rooms or their nighttime tasks. China went to the kitchen to make a cup of tea to take upstairs and found Brian and Janet there, having one of their verbal sparring matches. Wanting to give them privacy, she decided against the tea and went outside through the library and onto the porch.

The night was warm and quiet and smelled of apples.

"Where are you going?" It was a simple question that shouldn't annoy her, but it was spoken by Campbell, and so it did. All she wanted was a moment's peace, not another reminder that when she left here, her heart and soul would stay.

She sat down on the top step. "Nowhere," she replied a little sharply. "I just wanted some air."

HE DIDN'T LIKE her tone. He also didn't like the look in her eyes, as if she was no longer part of the picture, as if she'd soon be gone. She had every right to her feelings of dispossession, but he didn't understand why loving him, and his loving her, didn't make her feel that she belonged here.

It irritated him that he'd been on the Jasper's Camp School's Web site—pleasantly surprised that such a small school had one—hoping to locate the mysterious ZS and find out if he was China's father. Hopefully, he could answer some questions for her that would make her feel connected to her past and less determined to leave Shepherd's Knoll.

He'd been elated to find a Zachary Sherman in the

lineup of students and further elated when he turned out to be the right age. One classmate had had an e-mail address for him and Campbell had written, deciding not to pull punches. Time was short. He needed desperately to keep China here, and felt sure only the imminent arrival of her father could do that.

He explained to Sherman about China's search for her parents, and the discovery that her mother had died all those years ago. He told him about the ring and the inscription inside. He gave him his name and the address and phone number at Shepherd's Knoll, as well as his cell number. He'd pleaded with him to call if he could add anything to the mystery of China's parentage, explained that he loved her very much, and while he didn't care who her parents were, she didn't seem able to move on without knowing.

That had been three days ago, and so far, no reply. Campbell was beginning to conclude that either Zachary Sherman wasn't her father, or if he was, then for reasons of his own, he didn't want to admit it.

In either case, Campbell had few options left. He sat down beside her on the step. "When are you leaving?" he asked. He knew the question was counterproductive, but he was cranky.

She was quiet for a moment, then replied, "As soon as it's right."

"It'll never be right."

"You know what I mean."

"No, I don't. I don't understand you at all. Can't you just put aside what you don't have and deal with what's right here?"

"Cam…" Her tone sounded warning.

"No," he said. "I'm not going to let you leave without a fight. I want you to stay. The family wants you to stay. You could find out every detail about your past and never have the kind of love you have here."

"I know that," she said forcefully, "and I love all of you, too. But I'd never be sure…"

"I don't *care* about that," he interrupted, catching her arm when she would have gotten to her feet. "You love me, and for the moment it's because I'm a way into the family you thought was yours, but even if that was true, I wouldn't care. I love you and if you gave me a week, I'd make you the happiest woman this side of heaven."

"Yes, you would," she said, the tears in her eyes gleaming in the moonlight. "But I'd make you a miserable man."

"I'll risk it."

"I won't let you."

He couldn't help the huff of exasperation. "Jeez! Where did you get this idea that you're in charge of protecting my future? And while we're at it, stop trying to turn yourself into some tragic figure who'd corrupt my life with your grief. You've had everything! Adoptive parents who loved you, a sister who's the dearest, nicest—"

"She's *your* sister!" she shouted at him.

That surprised him a little. Was there some problem here he wasn't understanding? "She's still your sister in every way that's important. And if she chooses to make a life with us, well, then, we'd share her. Ah, I get it, since you can't have your life with us, or think you can't, you don't want to give up your life with her."

"I *do* want to give it! That's why I'm leaving."

"That's giving, not sharing. There's a subtle but important difference. You'll let us have her, but you won't stay to be part of it?"

She put both hands to her eyes. "Campbell, I...just can't get over this feeling that I don't belong anywhere. I feel lost and a little crabby, and I don't want you to have to deal with that when you finally have your sister back."

He wanted to shake her and tell her to just get over it, but he knew such a tactic would be useless. So he continued to reason. "You belong with me!" He tried to inject that with a note of authority she would respect. "And I can't imagine you're going to get in the way of my relationship with Janby."

She looked up at him with a watery smile. "Janby. I guess it's a good thing I'm not Abby. Chinby just doesn't have the same ring to it."

He caught her hand and pulled her to her feet. "Come on. You're staying with me tonight."

"Cam..."

"Shush."

The downstairs was quiet when he led her back inside and up the stairs. They could hear Killian and Cordie talking in Killian's room, and quiet music came from Janet's. He pushed his way into his room and pulled her in after him, then closed it. He leaned against it with a sigh, relieved they hadn't been seen. Though he didn't mind anyone knowing he intended to sleep with her tonight, he didn't want anything to delay that.

The room was dark and warm, and he crossed the carpet to push open a window. The smell of apples wafted in.

"I want to stay tonight," she said softly as he came back to her, "but it's to say goodbye."

He kissed her without comment. *You've got another thing coming, lady,* he wanted to say, but if she was happy believing that...

"Cam…" She tried to make him understand between kisses that she was serious, but he kissed harder and longer than she could speak, so they finally lay entangled on the bed, argument ceased in favor of lovemaking.

He did everything in his power to demonstrate the depth and breadth of his love for her. He was traditional and imaginative, and when she responded with ardor in her own creative way, he enjoyed her assumption of control and considered it a sign that she wasn't as ready to leave as she thought she was.

Later, when she lay wrapped in his arms and he felt her tears against his throat, he was convinced she wouldn't leave.

Chapter Thirteen

Campbell stood on a ladder, helping China string Japanese lanterns in preparation for the party the following day. Killian had gone to the city, and Sawyer, who was visiting a prospective client of the foundation, also in the city, had ridden in with Killian.

Brian's shipment had finally arrived, and he'd gone to the store to receive it and restock his shelves. Daniel had driven Chloe, Cordie and Janet to town on a shopping expedition.

The men working on the addition had taken the day off to repair a problem in the choir loft of the old church in Losthampton, but promised to be back the following day. Work was going well, and the framing was up. Chloe was pleased with their progress and hadn't protested the delay.

"Sawyer and Sophie will be married in the old church," she'd said with a Gallic shrug. "We don't want anyone falling through the choir loft."

"I took a call today from the travel agent," Campbell said to China, attaching a colorful paper lantern to the thin wire stretched from tree to tree in the backyard, "confirming your flight home tomorrow afternoon."

She'd intended to tell him that she'd made arrangements to leave, but she hadn't found the right moment. The family was so loud and cheerful and ever-present that private time had been almost impossible to find. And the nights…

She had told him over and over in the two weeks since Janet's positive DNA report arrived that she'd promised his mother she'd stay for the party, then she had to go back to work to take up her own life. Of course, she'd slept in his arms every night since then, too, so he may very well have convinced himself she wasn't serious.

In fact, she *was* having second thoughts, but she knew that was an emotional reaction to the rampant good cheer at Shepherd's Knoll, the happy sense of belonging she saw in Janet—or Janby, as everyone now called her. Who wouldn't want to stay and be a part of it?

But on a rational level, ignoring her feelings, she followed through with her plans to leave and did what she knew to be best for all concerned. Janet needed time alone with the Abbotts, and Campbell should assume the post in Florida and find himself. Despite how happy China had been here, she just had to accept that it wasn't her life.

"I was going to tell you after the party," she said.

"Nice of you," he replied. He climbed down the ladder, moved it several feet, then climbed it again, all the time avoiding her eyes. He reached down for the lantern she offered up.

"Campbell, try to understand," she pleaded. She noticed that ignoring emotion to operate on logic had a curiously painful effect.

"Sorry. I can't." He gave the lantern a small push and watched it sway, making sure it was well attached.

"You want everyone to understand why *you* have to work on another estate," she reminded him reasonably, stepping back while he climbed down again to move the ladder. "Why is my situation any different?"

"Because I'm trying to find out about myself." He climbed up again. "You're running *away* from yourself."

"What?" she demanded.

"You asked."

"Campbell, I'm trying to protect you from—"

He snatched the lantern from her. "Oh, give me a break. You're protecting you. So you lost your mother and you don't know who your father was. It's sad, but it shouldn't ruin your life. The unfortunate truth is that the world is full of people suffering the same thing, but they're doing the best they can with who they are. Or are you afraid somehow you can't be a worthwhile woman on your own? I hate to tell you this when you're so set on feeling deprived, but you're a charming, exciting and downright remarkable woman all by yourself. So for God's sake, live up to your potential."

She gasped in indignation at that brutal appraisal of her position. The temptation to knock the ladder out from under him was almost overwhelming. She settled for smacking his leg, instead.

"If that's your take on my life, I'm happy I'm flying out of yours!"

He hung the lantern. "Actually you're not. I canceled your booking."

Her mouth formed the word *what* again, but her anger was so strong all that came out was a squeak.

She was reconsidering knocking the ladder out from under him when she heard the gunshots. Four loud pops in rapid succession, followed by shouts, then more gunfire.

Campbell stiffened and turned in the direction of the sound, looking out over the treetops. After a moment, he scrambled down, leaping the last few steps, and pointed her toward the house.

"Go inside!" he shouted at her as he ran in the direction of the sound. "Lock yourself in!"

She did as he directed, her heart pounding. Her brain was wiped clean of their argument as she tried to deal with the reality of gunshots on this sunny afternoon. An ugly dread stole over her, bringing back memories of that night in the orchard when someone had set the Duchess on fire, then struck her down.

She locked the kitchen door after her. She called Kezia's name, then remembered that she'd gone home early today. Tomorrow was going to be a long day for her, and Killian and Sawyer were bringing back pizza tonight so that she had the evening off.

She ran around the house locking doors, trying not to panic. Tante Bijou always sat in her room upstairs in the afternoon, watching television. She wouldn't disturb her unless she had to.

When every door and window was as secure as she could make them, she went to the kitchen window and looked out, watching for some sign that the noise had been something innocuous. Any moment now, Campbell would come up the driveway, a smile on his face, to tell her the sounds they'd mistaken for gunshots had simply been children with firecrackers.

She watched and waited.

CAMPBELL RACED to the perimeter where Winfield's men were posted and, to his horror, found no one there. He scanned the grounds in the direction of the shots, then was suddenly knocked to the ground from behind. He swung back with his elbow, as his attacker tried to hold him down and connected with something solid. He heard an "oof!" of pain, then as he swung again, a whispered "Mr. Campbell!"

It was Winfield's voice. "Stay down! We've got somebody in the orchard, but we don't know how many there are."

Winfield lay beside him on his stomach and they watched a commotion in the trees nearest the road. There was shouting as branches moved wildly and a body dressed in camouflage came flying onto the road as though thrown. It was followed quickly by another, and then a third.

Four of Winfield's men came out of the woods, rifles trained on the bodies struggling to their feet.

Campbell rose and would have started for the road, but Winfield caught his arm and yanked him back. "I've got the gun!" he snapped at him. "You stay behind me!"

More impressed than offended by the man's warrior mode, Campbell swept a hand out, inviting him to go first.

The men in camouflage were really boys, eighteen or nineteen, Campbell guessed. He thought he recognized one of them from the Bunker, a teen hangout the Abbott Mills Foundation supported to keep kids off the street. He'd been shot in the arm and was bleating like a sheep.

Winfield went to inspect the arm. "Just a flesh wound," he said, looking angrily into the boy's face. "You can stop crying."

The boy tried manfully to pull it together but didn't seem able to. His friends, hands held behind their backs by Winfield's men, looked at one another in disgust at their cohort's anguish.

"Crap, Willie," the taller of the two said. "Shut up. They can hear you in Jersey."

"Well, you get shot!" the boy wept. "See how you like it!"

"What are you guys doing," Winfield asked quietly, "shooting at my men?"

Willie continued to whine. The other two looked away.

Winfield turned to one of his men. "Call the police," he said. "Tell them we have three attempted-murder suspects."

"Murder?" Willie asked, finally managing to stop crying.

"You shot at my men," Winfield answered. "That's attempted murder."

"No, it wasn't!" Willie denied. He looked first at one cohort, then the other. Even they were looking a little nervous.

"We…we…"

"Willie!" the tall one warned.

"You can get life for attempted murder, you know," Winfield said.

"We weren't trying to kill anybody!" Willie insisted.

"What *were* you trying to do?"

Willie's face began to crumple. The third boy cleared his throat. "We were hunting," he said with a remarkably straight face. "For…" He looked to his friend for help.

"Possum!" he replied.

Winfield snorted scornfully. "Get these guys out of here!"

"Wait!" Willie said as Winfield's men began to haul them away. Winfield held up a hand to make them stop.

"You want to tell me the truth, Willie? Who sent you here?"

"That old Girard guy," he blurted. "He paid us big to make a distortion. It wasn't attempted murder."

Winfield frowned. "A what?"

"A *distraction*, you idiot!" the third boy said.

It took Campbell just about three seconds to realize what that meant. He started for the house at a run.

IT HAD BEEN TEN MINUTES and China hadn't seen any-one or heard a sound coming from the direction of the gunshots. She considered going out to check but decid-ed against it, unwilling to leave Tante Bijou alone on the chance the sounds had really been gunshots.

She worried about Campbell, wondered what the si-lence was all about. She remembered their conversation in the yard and would have done anything to take it back. If he'd been hurt because he thought she was anxious to leave him, she'd never forgive herself.

She went through the quiet house to the library and looked out the French doors for some sign of activity, but there was nothing. Only the bright blue sky, sunshine on the leaves of the apple trees, a slight breeze stirring them.

Still, she couldn't get over a sense of foreboding. The house, usually so full of activity and conversation, was quiet as a crypt. She shuddered at her own analogy.

She reminded herself that the house was quiet because the usually fun filled people who inhabited it were out doing fun things. Cordie was shopping for summer shoes; Chloe and Janet were having their hair done. It cheered China to think about them having fun in town while she wandered the empty house, waiting for Campbell to come and tell her everything was all right.

She went back toward the kitchen, thinking she'd make a pot of tea for her and Tante Bijou. She was in the central hallway when she caught the smell of smoke.

Her first thought was that she'd already put on the kettle and forgotten to fill it, but she knew that wasn't true. She didn't want to believe that the gunshots had been real, that Campbell was in danger, that Shepherd's Knoll was in jeopardy.

She followed the smell, her heartbeat accelerating as the odor grew more and more acrid. She heard the active crackle of flames even before she saw them. Some horrid need to see what she was up against drove her toward the sound and the smell.

She rounded the corner of the living room and saw

the entire sunporch addition completely engulfed in flames. The raw lumber fed it and, as she stared dumbly, a drum of something in the collection of tools and materials in one corner exploded and blew open the window wall that had been cut out of the library. The draperies caught, and fire roared along the ceiling toward the hallway.

"China?" The sound of Tante Bijou's voice spurred her to action.

She turned back the way she'd come and ran up the stairs to the second-floor bedrooms. Tante Bijou sat at the top in her wheelchair, her sweet, wrinkled face further furrowed in concern. *"Je sens le feu?"* she said. I smell fire?

"Oui!" China replied, trying to think quickly. She considered trying to get Tante Bijou's chair down the stairs before the fire took hold, then dismissed that idea. She wasn't sure she was strong enough to control the wheelchair without losing it.

She quickly turned the wheelchair around and ran it toward the turret bedroom that opened out onto a full balcony. On the side of the house opposite the addition, it was so far free of fire, though she could see billows of dark smoke. She had to get Tante Bijou to fresh air while she decided what to do.

"Attendez ici," she said. "Wait here, and I'm going to get the ladder. *Et je vais chercher l'échelle,"* she repeated in French.

She ran back through the bedroom and the hallway, headed for the stairway, her breath catching in her throat when she saw smoke wafting up. But no fire was visible yet, so she held her breath and ran down the stairs, down the hall and out the front door. If she kept Tante Bijou between her body and the rung of the ladder, she might be able to get her down safely.

Her breath exploded from her as she ran out into the fresh air and saw Campbell racing toward her. She'd never been so glad to see anyone in her life. Even as her heart told her she'd been an idiot, that she'd made problems for herself where there weren't any, that he loved her and whatever she knew or didn't know about her past didn't matter a damn, she diverted her path toward the ladder.

He ran to her, catching her arms. "Are you hurt? What happened?"

"Tante Bijou!" she said urgently, pointing to the porch where the old lady waved at them like a member of a royal family greeting her subjects on a national holiday.

They could hear the roar of the flames on the other side of the house, and the smoke now rose in a high, dark column.

Winfield joined them and together they carried the ladder to the house.

"It isn't tall enough!" Winfield said, as it stood several feet short of the bottom of the balcony.

"Put it up against the pillar," Campbell said, pulling it in that direction. "I'll be able to climb down the pillar until I can reach the ladder. That old clematis vine is like steel."

Winfield tried to push him out of the way. "I'll do it."

"Get serious, Winfield." Campbell pushed back. "I'm younger and more agile."

"Isn't that touching?" A new voice injected itself into the urgency of the moment with a venomous note.

China turned in surprise to see an older man in brown designer pants and shirt carrying a—she had to look twice!—blowtorch. The pointed nozzle spewed flame. The expression on his face was filled with hatred and chilling purpose. Two burly young men stood behind him.

"The young master and the servant fighting over who should take the risk." He'd said that almost pleasantly, but now his expression and his voice hardened. He pointed the nozzle of the torch at Campbell. "There's enough risk for all of you. Get in the house."

"Corbin," Campbell said calmly, pulling China to his side. "There's a helpless old woman up there in a wheelchair."

The two young men with Corbin looked up at Tante Bijou, clinging to the railing in her wheelchair, then looked at each other.

Corbin? China tried to remember where she'd heard that name before, and then it came to her; Corbin Girard was Brian's father. Brian's *estranged* father

Corbin blew air scornfully. "There's no such thing as a helpless Abbott. Even an old woman. Inside!"

"She's not an Abbott," Campbell said, moving subtly to shield China. Winfield moved with him. The men with Corbin grew more alert. "She's my mother's aunt. Come on, Corbin. Even you aren't evil enough to leave an old woman in a burning house."

"But I am." He replied evenly, with apparently no qualms of conscience. He aimed the blowtorch at them. "Get in the house! Brian prevented me from getting at

Abbott Mills, then I thought—" He sighed now and spoke with boredom. "You're all so sickeningly devoted to one another. And Killian's a smart man. If I destroyed the company, he'd have it on its feet again in a year. But if I destroy the house and members of the family, your family will never heal. They'll remember me till their dying breaths."

"Why would you want to do that?" China asked in horror.

"Because the Abbotts destroyed me." He replied almost pleasantly. "I had everything until Susannah Abbott threw herself at me. Then little by little, my life eroded. My wife hated me, but I still had to raise the boy, the November Corporation was always second to Abbott Mills, and that boy, who cost me all those years, went over to your side the first chance he got. You took Brian, so I think it's only fair that I get one of you."

His eyes were wild. "If you don't get in the house right now," he threatened Campbell, "I'll make a torch of your woman's hair!"

Without warning, Winfield sprang at him and they fell together, shouting invectives

At the same moment, Campbell aimed himself at the two young men, and they all went down in a kicking, flailing pile.

There was a scream of pain and Corbin stood over Winfield, who clutched a hand to a wound on his chest. There was a hole the size of a saucer in the front of his shirt, its edges and the skin underneath charred from the torch.

Campbell was on his feet again, but Corbin swung

the blowtorch at him, a smirk on his lips broadcasting his intention.

China lost all thought and threw herself at him at a run, striking him on the shoulder as hard as she could. They fell together into a bed of pansies. The blowtorch landed harmlessly in the rocks that bordered the garden.

She heard Corbin's gasp of surprise, Winfield's shout of her name and Campbell's round curse. Then Campbell was hauling her off Corbin as the two thugs who'd accompanied him seemed uncertain about what to do.

China braced herself to take one or both of them on, when a large, round terra-cotta bowl fell from above and landed squarely on the head of one of the men. He sank to the grass, the broken pot of French thyme beside him.

His companion looked up to see where the missile had come from. Tante Bijou dusted off her hands and shouted something in French for which there was no direct English translation—at least not a decent one.

The second man turned and ran, only to be intercepted by two of Winfield's men. Another stood over a now unconscious Corbin Girard while another helped steady the ladder as Campbell climbed it, stretched from it to the porch, then scrambled over the railing.

He put Tante Bijou over his shoulder and stepped over the railing to reverse his path.

Someone had called the fire department, the police and an ambulance. Men in uniform were everywhere. Shouting excitedly in French, Tante Bijou was placed on a gurney. The paramedic looked at China in confusion.

"She's telling you that she's fine, but that Winfield is burned." China pointed to the Abbotts' chief of security, who was on his feet, a hand clutched to the burn on his chest as he directed his men to aim garden hoses at the fire. "But, please. Check her over anyway."

Then she noticed that the family was home, standing in shock at the side of the house, watching the crowd, eyes widening at the mess. Then Killian, Sawyer and Daniel, dressed in their business suits, raced to help. Chloe hurried to Tante Bijou on the gurney, and Janet had an arm around Cordie.

China hurried to them to explain what had happened.

"Have you seen Versace?" Cordie asked her worriedly.

China shook her head. "I'm sorry, Cordie. I sort of had my hands full with Tante Bijou."

"Of course." She started resolutely toward the house.

China caught her arm. "Where are you going?"

"Lately, he's always in Campbell's office," she said. "I'm just going to—"

The words hadn't left her mouth when Killian walked out in his shirtsleeves, the cat struggling to free itself from his arms. "He's fine," he told Cordie, who began crooning over him, a wide smile on her face. He was on the top shelf of Campbell's bookcase. I want you to know that the three of us risked life and limb to get him down."

She kissed his cheek. "Thank you, darling. How bad is it inside?"

"The addition's gone," he said with a philosophical shrug, "but except for the time and effort invested in it, only lumber was destroyed. The library and that end of the hall have a lot of smoke and fire damage, and everything's going to smell bad for a while, but most of the house is fine." He grinned. "The upstairs and the kitchen weren't even touched. That makes me happy."

Chloe joined them and wrapped her arms around China. She stepped back to look into her face, her eyes stunned and filled with—China thought she had to be deluding herself—a mother's love.

"Tante Bijou told me that you fought for Campbell like a wild woman. That you knocked Corbin Girard to the ground when he threatened him with a blowtorch."

She had, hadn't she. She'd had an epiphany in the past half hour. But she wasn't particularly interested in praise.

"Tante Bijou dropped your pot of French thyme from the balcony on one of his henchmen's heads. Knocked him out cold. It was a wonderful thing to see."

Despite China's smile, Chloe continued to look serious. "She said you risked your life to get her to safety, then ran back outside to get the ladder and would have tried to save her yourself, except that Campbell and Winfield came back."

"That's China," Janet said, wrapping her in a hug. "Completely selfless when it comes to people she loves."

Killian kissed her cheek. "So, you saved two members of the family. Thank you." He pointed across the yard at Campbell, directing firefighting operations. "And for someone who claims to feel as though he doesn't belong, he sure fights awfully hard for the place."

"MR. ABBOTT!" Ben Fuller, Losthampton's fire chief, took hold of Campbell's garden hose and fixed him with a firm look. "This is our job and we know what we're doing. I understand that you run this estate, but I've had twenty-eight years with the department. It's better to have only one chief at a fire."

Campbell relinquished the hose. "I'm sorry," he said. "I got a little caught up in the moment."

"Of course you did. It's your home. But we've got it under control and I'll take it from here."

Campbell spotted his family across the lawn and went to join them. The police had pulled China aside and he started toward her to help her answer questions, but his mother waylaid him.

She embraced him tearfully.

"*Maman,* I'm fine," he said firmly, holding Chloe close so that she would see he was telling the truth.

"I've been listening to China talking to the police, and Tante Bijou told me what she saw." She clutched him more tightly. "When I think of what could have happened."

"I know, but it didn't."

"*Ma tante* says China fought for you."

"Yes, she did."

"So you're going to take her with you when you go?" Chloe stepped back to look into his eyes, her own serene now that she knew her family was safe and whole. Like a good mother, she wanted for him whatever he wanted for himself.

"No, I'm not," he said.

At her look of disappointed surprise, he pinched her cheek. "I'm going to stay here and see that she stays with me. Excuse me, *maman*. I have to give her hell for the risks she took today."

Campbell went to where she stood with the police and helped her answer their questions. He had to talk to his brothers about it, but he wasn't sure that prosecuting Girard was a good idea—because of Brian. Still, he'd seen the look in the man's eyes. Old bitterness and anger, long stored and fermenting, had turned Corbin Girard into a truly demented man. Campbell didn't want to take the chance that he'd ever pose a threat to the family again.

When the police were finished, Campbell looked around for a quiet place to talk with China. But the place was still crawling with firemen and Winfield's crew. One of them had rescued Tante Bijou's wheelchair from the balcony, and she now sat it in under a shady maple. Kezia had spread blankets and brought out cold drinks and snacks for the family.

Campbell caught China's arm and led her after him toward the boathouse. She looked exhausted and sort of…stunned. And the hand he held shook a little bit.

He sat her on the old sofa rescued from his mother's renovation of the living room.

She looked at him as though he was a stranger, and that shook his confidence in what he intended to tell her. But in this family of poster boys for self-confidence…

"You took a lot of foolish chances today," he said, stuffing a coffee filter in the coffeemaker basket. He found the canister of French Roast and measured out enough for a pot.

She lost that vague look and focused on him with a sudden firming of her lips. "Did I?" she asked coolly.

He slid the basket in place, poured water into the well, then turned on the switch. "You did." He went to sit beside her. "You attacked a man threatening you with a blowtorch."

"Correction," she said. "I attacked a man threatening *you* with a blowtorch."

"Which bring us to my point."

"And that is?"

"Do you have any idea what he could have done to you with that thing?" He posed the question quietly, but he remembered the absolute terror he'd felt when he'd watched her fling herself at Corbin Girard.

She arched an eyebrow in royal resentment of his interrogation. "My concern was what he could have done to *you* with it."

He nodded gravely. "And so we must ask ourselves: do your actions sound like those of a woman who would marry a man simply to gain entry to his family? Or are they more indicative of a woman so in love with a man she'd risk her own life to protect him from being flambéed?"

She socked him in the shoulder. "Feeling pretty smug, aren't we?"

"We are," he admitted. "And loved."

She looked into his eyes and he saw that same serenity his mother had worn. "Me, too," she said with a smile. "I'll go with you to Florida."

"No," he said without thinking, then saw that serenity change to horrified disbelief. It had been flatteringly quick, but he never wanted her to doubt his adoration of her. He caught her hands. "No, I'm not going to Flor-

ida. I'm staying here. I want you to *stay* here with me.
I belong here. You belong here."

She fell into his arms and held on.

His only regret about all this, he thought later as he
made love to her on the old sofa, was that he'd never had
a response from Zachary Sherman. The man might have
been her father or he might not, but at least Campbell
could have told China he'd tried to find him for her.
Without a reply, he thought it best to keep the whole
thing to himself.

Still, what a day it had been. Someone had been listening to his prayers.

Chapter Fourteen

The following day, every member of the Abbott family helped prepare for the party. Chloe insisted they have it despite the damage, because welcoming Abby home was something she'd dreamed about for twenty-five years. She gave instructions to simply close off the fire-damaged south end of the house and hired a cleaning company to get rid of the smoke smell.

"Most of the party will be outdoors, anyway," she said, glowing with good cheer, a silk designer scarf wrapped around her hair to protect it.

With everyone home, they had breakfast in the dining room with the French doors open to the outside. Brian had come to the house yesterday afternoon to investigate the source of the smoke he'd seen and been stricken that his father had done such a thing. Brian had accompanied his father to the police department despite Corbin's loud and persistent claims that he didn't want him. Sawyer had gone with Brian to provide moral support.

They'd come home for dinner, Sawyer looking angry

and Brian sitting quietly, clearly troubled. When the children had left the table and gone upstairs to watch a movie, Killian leaned across the table toward Brian.

"You can share with us if you want to," he'd said. "We can guess how hard all this is for you. In fact, we've been talking about it, and we won't press charges if—"

"You have to press charges," Brian had interrupted. "He was willing to kill people today! And he used a bunch of troubled kids to help pull off his plan." He shook his head in disbelief. "How sick is that? If he's prosecuted, maybe he'll get some help." He'd sighed and added grimly, "I'm so sorry that happened."

"There's no reason for you to feel responsible," Sawyer had said. "We bullied you into coming over to our side. His problems are his own."

Brian had accepted that with a nod.

He seemed a little more cheerful this morning. He even managed to harass Janby, who seemed to take great pleasure in returning the favor.

After breakfast, Chloe assigned everyone chores. Campbell and China were the last to receive their instructions. "Please weed the flower boxes on the back porch," she said, "and do your best to repair the flower bed into which China threw Corbin Girard." She hugged her. "Bless you for doing that."

While Campbell went to the gardening shed for the tools, China busied herself with the box of yellow and orange nasturtiums on the porch railing. She looked up at the sound of a car and saw a dusty red compact pulling up near the steps. It had Massachusetts plates.

She was wondering if Chloe had invited guests from that far away when a middle-aged man of average height climbed out of the car and slowly approached the porch. She gave him a friendly smile.

He stared at her a moment. His eyes were hazel, his hair close cropped and dark, and graying in a small patch over his left eye.

"Good morning," she said.

He continued to stare, then he made a curiously nervous gesture with one hand. It went to his heart, then to his mouth, then back down to his side again.

"Can I help you?" she asked.

"I'm…I'm looking for…" He took a sheet of paper out of his pocket and consulted it. "Campbell Abbott," he said.

"He'll be right along," China told him. "He's just gone to the garden shed for some tools. Would you like to come up onto the porch and wait?" She indicated the wicker rockers behind her.

He couldn't seem to take his eyes off her. And it wasn't a troublesome stare, but a sort of fascination she didn't understand. She'd thought when she'd brushed her hair this morning that the bathroom mirror had framed the face of a woman aglow with love. But she didn't think it would be apparent to anyone else, particularly a stranger.

He shook his head, clearly awed by Shepherd's Knoll. "I…think I'd better wait," he said, remaining at the bottom of the steps. "This is…quite a beautiful home. But you had a fire?"

"Yes. Fortunately, no major damage. An addition

was just getting under way, but the builder will start again tomorrow."

She went back to picking weeds, glancing up at the stranger as she worked, his fascination inspiring her own. "The house intimidated me when I first came," she said, liking his shy manner, wanting him to feel comfortable. "But the Abbotts are a wonderful family. Are you a friend?"

"Ah...no."

"But you know Campbell?"

He waved the sheet of paper he held. "I just received some correspondence from him."

Campbell came around the side of the house, several small tools in his hand. "All *right!*" Campbell said. "Kezia's making caramel pecan brownies, and the first team finished with their chores gets to eat every—" He stopped mid-sentence when he noticed the stranger. He stared, an unusual hesitancy in his manner.

"Mr. Abbott?" the stranger asked.

"Yes," Campbell replied, setting the tools down on the bottom step.

The man offered his hand. "Zack Sherman."

"Are you really?" Campbell said softly, then shook his hand. "I mean...the details I gave you. Is it...you?"

China heard him swallow from up on the porch. "Yes," he said. "It's me."

Campbell hugged him. China stared at the two of them, wondering what on earth was going on. Then Campbell, wearing a wide smile, took the man's arm and led him up the stairs. Zack Sherman looked terrified. Still fascinated, but terrified.

"I'll get you two something to dr—" She reached for the door.

"No." Campbell caught her arm in his free hand. "We need you here."

"For what?"

Campbell smiled at Sherman. "Go ahead."

Sherman shook his head.

"Come on," Campbell chided gently. "You've come all this way."

"Do you have something to tell me?" China asked, trying to help. She put a hand on the man's arm as she spoke. He looked down at her fingers and a large tear rolled down his cheek.

Her heart punched against her rib cage.

"Bad news?" she asked. What could it be? she wondered, holding off panic. Her adoptive parents were gone, her sister was safely inside the house, there was no one else…

Finally he said in a hesitant voice, his eyes filled with pain and still…that fascination, "You're Margaret Roberts's daughter?"

Oh, my God. She thought. *Oh, my God!* No. It couldn't be. No one knew who he was, much less where he was!

"I'm your father," he said on a gasp of emotion. His voice shaking, he added, "You…look so much…like her."

She couldn't breathe. Emotion was building inside her like a class-five hurricane. Everything was beginning to rattle. She reached a hand out for Campbell and he caught it. He held on to her while she stared at the very nice, unassuming face of the man who'd just shaken her world off its axis.

"Maggie and I were friends in high school," he said. "But in the summer between our junior and senior year, we fell in love. Not very smart, but very much in love. She was so excited that she was pregnant. I had a job at the market and she was a teller at the bank and we had big plans for making a home for you. But when her parents found out about you, they sent her away to an aunt up in northern Canada somewhere. In the wilderness."

China's brain soaked up the words, desperate to make sense of them, to understand that he was explaining her life to her. "They didn't intend to be cruel," he said. "I know they loved her very much. Anyway, I joined the navy, thinking that I'd get my education, save some money and find a way to make a home for us when we were old enough."

He expelled that gasp of emotion again. "Then, while I was serving in Germany, I got a letter from a friend who told me that she died in an auto accident with her parents. But nobody knew what had happened to the baby. My commanding officer called around for me, trying to find out, but by the time we tracked you down, you'd been placed with the Grants. I still had two more years to serve, and it seemed like a cruelty to take you away from a family that had chosen you when I had nothing better to offer. So I left you there."

He burst into sobs and China, responding on instinct, wrapped her arms around him. They cried together.

"I prayed for a miracle," he finally said, "and then I got this letter from Mr. Abbott. I'm a long-haul trucker, that's why I didn't answer you right away. Oh, there are ways to keep in touch on the road, but I like not having to do that."

"There were initials in the ring your mother left," Campbell explained to China, "MR and ZS. We knew your mother had gotten pregnant in high school, so I presumed your father might be a classmate of hers. And I thought the Z was unusual enough that if I could find the school Web site, I might be able to find the man who had those initials."

"You did that for me?" she whispered, overwhelmed.

"Why are you surprised?" he asked. "I'd alter time for you, if I could. Fix the past. But I can't, so I just tried to put your future on the right track."

She threw her arms around him, so full of love and hope she thought she might erupt. After a moment she noticed that the entire family was crowded in the doorway, listening shamelessly.

Janet came out to take Zack Sherman's arm. "I'm your daughter's sister," she said. Then she laughed lightly. "That's one of those statements that requires a little explanation. "And these nosey parkers—" she indicated the Abbotts in the doorway "—are Campbell's family. I've been asked to invite you inside to have coffee and visit for a while."

"Um…"

"There's a big party here tonight. Which is odd, because there was a big fire here yesterday, but nothing stops a celebration at Shepherd's Knoll."

China thought her father…her father!…looked as though he was already wondering what he'd gotten himself into.

Chloe stepped out onto the porch to take his other arm. She and Janet escorted him inside and China could hear introductions under way as she remained on the porch, gazing into Campbell's loving eyes.

"Thank you," she whispered, "for understanding how much I needed that."

"You're welcome."

"Fifteen minutes ago," she said, looping her arms around his neck, "I loved you with the power of the sun."

"Wow." He kissed her lips.

"But now, my love is…" She hesitated. "There isn't a word big enough, forceful enough."

He entwined his fingers in her hair. "Then save your breath," he whispered, lowering his mouth to hers, "and just show me what you mean."

* * * * *

Welcome to the world of American Romance!
Turn the page for excerpts from our June 2005 titles.

BELONGING TO BANDERA by Tina Leonard

THE MOMMY WISH by Pamela Browning

AN ENGAGEMENT OF CONVENIENCE
by Mollie Molay

SARAH'S GUIDE TO LIFE, LOVE & GARDENING
by Connie Lane

We hope you enjoy every one of these books!

Tina Leonard continues her popular COWBOYS BY THE DOZEN series with *Belonging to Bandera* (#1069). These books are wonderfully entertaining, fast-paced and exciting. If you've never read Tina Leonard, you're in for a treat. After all, who can resist a cowboy—let alone twelve of them! Watch for the tenth book, *Crockett's Seduction,* coming in September 2005.

Meet the brothers of Malfunction Junction and let the roundup of those Jefferson bad boys begin!

Bandera looked out the window as he and his brother, Mason, drove by the miles of their ranch. "We have one pretty spread of land. I'm going to miss Malfunction Junction."

"We're only going to be gone a few days," Mason said.

"Well, I like my little corner of the world just the way it is," Bandera said. "Hey, look at that!"

Bandera craned his head to look at the woman on the side of the road, waving a large sign. She was wearing blue-jean shorts and a white halter top. "Probably a car wash," he murmured. "Slow down, Mason."

"No," Mason said. "There's no time. This is going to be an information-seeking venture, not a woman-hunt. Nor do I need a car wash."

They whizzed past so fast Bandera could barely read her sign. The blonde flashed it at him, holding it up high, so that he got a dizzying look at her jiggling breasts, white teeth, laughing blue eyes and legs. She was so cute, he was sure the fanny she was packing was just as sweet. "Stop!" he yelled.

"No!" Mason said, stomping on the brake anyway. "Why couldn't you have stayed home?"

"Her sign says she needs assistance," Bandera said righteously, although he really thought it had read I'm Holly.

"And Lord only knows we never leave a lady without assistance." Mason glanced up into his mirror. "I sense trouble in a big way."

The lady bounced to Mason's truck door. "Hi," she said.

"Howdy," Mason and Bandera said together. "Can we help you, miss?" Bandera asked.

"I'm waiting for my cousin," she said.

Mason was silent. Bandera took off his hat. "Did your car break down, miss?"

"No." She smiled, and dimples as cute as baby lima beans appeared in her cheeks. Bandera felt his heart go *boom!*

"I'm getting picked up by my cousin," she said. "That's why my sign says I'm Holly."

"Nowhere on her bright white placard do I see the word *assistance,* Bandera. Or even *Help!*" Mason sent his brother a disgusted grimace.

"We haven't seen each other in a while," Holly said. "He might not recognize me."

"Okay," Mason said. "You'll have to pardon us. We need to be getting along. Normally, we don't stop for ladies holding signs, but we thought you needed help."

"Actually, I do," she said. "I could use a kiss."

Bandera's jaw dropped. "A kiss? Why?"

"I'm feeling dangerous," she explained, "Since I just caught my fiancé in bed with my best friend."

"Ouch," Mason said.

"Precisely. That's why I called my cousin. This is our prearranged meeting place."

"So you're running away," Mason said.

"I'm going on a well-needed sabbatical," she corrected him. "We were getting married tomorrow. I don't feel like hanging around for the tears. I have an itch to see the countryside."

"Actually, you have an itch to get as far away from your fiancé as possible," Mason theorized.

"You understand me totally."

"So about that kiss…" Bandera began, unable to resist.

This month, look for Pamela Browning's The Mommy Wish (#1070), from our "Fatherhood" series. As always, this author offers us a wonderful setting for this warm romance. A single father, his seven-year-old daughter and our heroine are temporarily stranded in the small town of Greensea Springs. In this unique Florida community, Molly Kate McBryde finds herself becoming attached to Eric Norvald's little girl…and to Eric.

Rain again. Cold and dreary, beating against the wide window of the great gray skyscraper housing the McBryde Industries corporate offices. And on the console in front of the window, a framed picture of Molly Kate McBryde and her grandfather, taken in a more salubrious climate, before she'd started this miserable job in this miserable building that always seemed engulfed in miserable weather.

"Your grandpa Emmett called," chirped her assistant, the cheery and irrepressible Mrs. Lorraine Brinkle of the short blond curls and flippy skirts.

Molly tossed her briefcase on the antique rolltop desk that had once been Emmett's. "I'd better call him back. How did he sound?"

"You know. Like always, and with that Irish brogue of his. Flirting shamelessly. Teasing me about wanting your job."

Molly grinned. "On days like today, you can have it. So much responsibility, so little time." She was Number-Two Honcho in Corporate Accounting, a position that had its trying moments.

"I didn't mean that the way it sounded," Mrs. Brinkle amended. "Anyway, I'm looking into a promotion to Legal."

Molly felt a prickle of apprehension. She didn't want to lose Lorraine Brinkle, a woman of many skills. Mrs. Brinkle had not only worked a stint as a legal secretary before she'd signed on at McBryde Industries, but she'd also been trained as a bookkeeper. On top of that, she had attended college at night for years before graduating with a degree in business six weeks ago at the age of forty-five.

"Oh, don't threaten me with Legal. We need you here," Molly said hastily.

"Mmm-hmm. But now that I've got my college degree, I'm ready for bigger and better things. That's what your grandfather says, anyway." Mrs. Brinkle rolled her eyes.

"What else did he say?"

"Only to call him," Mrs. Brinkle said. She scooped a stack of file folders off Molly's desk and winked. "He mentioned something about sending you to Florida."

Florida sounded like a good idea. This was the last week in October, and whitecaps were scuffing the chill gray surface of Lake Michigan, and this morning, Molly had discovered moth holes in last year's winter coat. She picked up the phone.

Her grandfather answered on the first ring. "Molly Kate," he said before she could say hello. "I want you and Patrick to sail *Fiona* to Fort Lauderdale."

"Um, Grandpa," Molly said. "I have a job. You hired me."

"How long ago was that? Seven years? Isn't it time you had a vacation?"

"I came to Maine this summer. We took *Fiona* to Nova Scotia, remember? A good time was had by all."

"Well, now *Fiona*'s getting refurbished and repaired in North Carolina. I can't take her to Florida myself because I'm having some medical tests."

"Tests?" Molly said, alarmed. Since their Nova Scotia voyage, Emmett had suffered a few spells of dizziness, which, considering his heart condition, was alarming, but she'd thought everything was under control now that he was on medications.

"Oh, you know how it is. Doctors like to help out other doctors, so they're sending me to Minneapolis, where a new team of doctors will probably send me to some more doctors."

"Grandpa, you're scaring me."

"I hope I can scare off those doctors, as well. I want the boat in Florida when I get there, though."

"If I run off on this junket to Florida, who's going to look after things here?"

"Why, Mrs. Brinkle, of course. She's a go-getter, that one."

He was right. And keeping Lorraine Brinkle busy in Corporate Accounting would prevent her from pursuing an alternate destiny in the Legal Department until they could figure out some way to promote her to a job more in keeping with her many capabilities.

"I'll need to square it with Frank." Francis X. O'Toole was her boss, head of the department.

"I've already talked with him. You go with his blessing."

"Don't you think you should have let me broach the idea? Don't you think you're a bit too presumptuous, Grandpa dear?"

"Don't you think *you* protest too much, Molly dear?" Her grandfather's tone was teasing.

Molly sighed. "When do you want me to leave?"

"It'll most likely be the first of the week."

"Who's going to be my crew?"

"You are. I've hired a licensed captain who can help you get the boat to Fort Lauderdale."

"Who is it?"

"Never mind. Just…someone."

"A happy relationship requires that a woman make her man feel masculine…." And so begin the six rules created by sociologist Lucas Sullivan, who believes following these rules will lead to a happy marriage. But Lucas revised his "theory" after meeting April Morgan in *Marriage in Six Easy Lessons* (#1023) and now his best friend must as well! In the final book of the SULLIVAN RULES series, *An Engagement of Convenience* (#1071), Tom Eldridge learns that no relationship can be boiled down to rules—especially one with the spirited and sexy Lili Soulé. After all, these rules never said anything about women with two unruly young children….

"So, you're the one!"

At the sound of her boss's angry voice, Lili Soulé tried to cover the damning evidence in front of her. But it was too late to cover the draft of a flier demanding the management of the Riverview Building keep its child-care Center open.

To add to her alarm, the charcoal sketch she'd been

idly drawing was left in full view. If she wasn't already in trouble over her latest flier, she would be in deep trouble now.

Two years of working for Tom Eldridge, the publisher of *Today's World* magazine, where she worked as a graphic artist, hadn't diminished the crush she had on him. She been too shy to show it, but at moments like this the sound of his full baritone made her fingers ache to draw him, as she was caught doing now.

He was a man who took great pains to avoid socializing with his staff. He'd sounded friendly enough at weekly staff meetings, but he sure didn't sound friendly now.

Lili's heart raced as she turned to meet Tom's gaze. He was six feet of rugged masculinity, with a square jaw and, at the moment, angry chocolate-brown eyes. Heaven help her, he was grimly regarding her work on the drafting table. The frown that creased his forehead and the glow of fire in his eyes weren't helping Lili hold on to her courage. Still, now that her identity as the building's rabble-rouser was out in the open, she intended to put up a good defense. She nodded cautiously.

"So, you're the person who's been circulating fliers and a petition to keep the building's day-care Center open?"

"Yes," Lili replied, shaking slightly. "Someone has to do it."

"And, of course," he added wryly, "that someone had to be you?"

Lili didn't like the way Eldridge was looking at her, but the damage was done. If ever there was a time to assert herself and her right to free speech, that time was now. It was also time to forget how he unknowingly affected her.

"Yes. I have twins in after-school care. Someone had to do something to help convince the building's management to keep from closing the Center," she added in a defiant voice that not only seemed to surprise him, it surprised her, too.

Her boss's eyes narrowed. He pointed to the assignment sheet pinned to the corner of her drawing board. "I would have thought you'd be spending your time working on your assignment instead of spending your time stirring up trouble."

She gestured to a large sheet of drawing paper under the damning flier. "I started to, but another thought or two got in the way."

Eldridge motioned to the flier. "Yeah," he agreed grimly, "it sure looks as if *something* did get in the way. Like causing problems for everyone, including me."

Lili didn't intend to back off. The Center had provided tender, loving care for her twins for two years before they'd reached first grade. Now that the twins were in after-school care, keeping the Center open became more important than ever. She had to live with her conscience.

To Lili's dismay, he reached over and picked up the charcoal drawing she'd been working on. "What's this supposed to be? A wall target for you to shoot at?"

Lili wished she could fade into the woodwork. She was a mature woman, a single mother with twins, she told herself. Only an infatuated teenager drew pictures of a man who had captured her interest as this man had captured hers.

"No. I heard the sound of your voice and started drawing...." How could she tell Tom he was seldom far from her thoughts without sounding like a love-struck idiot?

Sarah's Guide to Life, Love and Gardening (#1072) is Connie Lane's third story to take place at the very romantic Cupid's Hideaway. If you had a chance to read Stranded at Cupid's Hideaway (#932) or Christmas at Cupid's Hideaway (#996) you'll remember some of the residents of South Bass Island, like the delightful Maisie, proprietor of the inn, and police chief Dylan O'Connell. If not, you'll enjoy meeting them for the first time—as Sarah does.

Connie Lane is a multi-published author who writes with genuine charm and humor. But there's wisdom that accompanies the wit, and characters who'll find a place in your heart. By the end of the book, you'll wish Cupid's Hideaway was a real place!

What is romance?
It's the question that Affairs of the Heart *viewers ask most often.*
Is romance about a look? A touch? Is it something as simple as the scent of lilacs wafting through an open doorway? Ah, if only it were as easy as that! But don't despair, dear reader. You have Sarah's Guide to Life, Love & Gardening. *And Sarah has all the answers.*
—Sarah's Guide to Life, Love & Gardening

"...until then, this is Sarah Allcroft of *Affairs of the*

Heart, wishing you beauty-filled days, elegant nights and a lifetime of romance."

Sarah held the smile. One second. Two seconds. Three.

"Cut!" Gino Felice, her director, gave her the thumbs-up and Sarah released the breath she was holding, along with the smile that cramped her face muscles and left her lips as dry as dust. Gino hurried over to where she was perched on a white wicker settee artfully accessorized with a dozen chintz pillows in a variety of colors and patterns. Flowers and checks, stripes and watercolor splashes, they all complemented her blush-pink linen suit to perfection. Sarah wouldn't have it any other way.

Gino kissed her cheek. "Gorgeous, darling. Your best show ever. One look at the tea you set this afternoon…" There was an assortment of adorable little canapés, finger sandwiches and cookies on a silver tray on the table in front of Sarah. Gino reached around the Limoges teapot and cups they'd borrowed from a local collector for the taping and grabbed a sandwich cut in the shape of a star. He popped the blackberry, sage and cream cheese concoction into his mouth, closed his eyes and smiled while he chewed.

"As soon as they see this episode, the good folks over at the Home & Hearth Network will jump up and take notice," he said. "They're going to want you in the fall lineup. I'd bet my silver-haired granny on it. I wouldn't be surprised if the phone started ringing with offers. Very soon."

Sarah wouldn't be surprised, either. Then again, there was little that ever surprised Sarah. She simply wouldn't allow it.

Her determination settled in the place that always felt jumpy before, during and after every taping and like it always did, it calmed Sarah and filled her with confidence.

By the time Becky Landis raced by to answer the phone that was ringing in the outer office, Sarah was smiling again.

"Good show, honey!" Becky was the producer, makeup artist and wardrobe mistress of *Affairs of the Heart*. She was also Sarah's best friend. She patted Sarah on the back as she zoomed by. "You got the directions for those knitted sachet bags, right?" she called over her shoulder. "I know we're going to get slammed by requests. Like we always do. And it's going to get crazier once we go national!" The last Sarah saw of her, an ear-to-ear grin was brightening Becky's expression.

Sarah knew exactly why. Once *Affairs of the Heart* was picked up for cable, she wasn't the only one whose star would rise. Becky would finally get the chance to work on a network show, just as she'd always dreamed. Gino and the rest of the crew would have the opportunity, at last, to use their considerable talents on a project more challenging than a shoestring-budget show with a tiny local audience.

Sarah, however, was the only one who was going to get thrust, pushed, dragged and swept into the limelight.

Her smile wilted and her insides started jumping all over again

One more taping out of the way.

One more bullet dodged.

Again.

She wondered how long she could keep it up.

AMERICAN *Romance*®

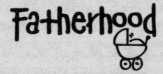

Fatherhood: what really defines a man.

It's the one thing all women admire in a man—
a willingness to be responsible for a child and
to care for that child with tenderness and love.

**Meet two men who are true fathers
in every sense of the word!**

Eric Norvald is devoted to his seven-year-old
daughter, Phoebe. But can he give her what she
really wants—a mommy? Find out in

Pamela Browning's
THE MOMMY WISH (AR #1070)

Available June 2005.

In

Laura Marie Altom's
TEMPORARY DAD (AR #1074),

Annie Harnesberry has sworn off men—especially
single fathers. But when her neighbor—a gorgeous
male—needs help with his triplet five-month-old
niece and nephews, Annie can't resist offering
her assistance.

Available July 2005.

www.eHarlequin.com   HARFATHER0505

If you enjoyed what you just read,
then we've got an offer you can't resist!

Take 2 bestselling love stories FREE!

Plus get a FREE surprise gift!

Clip this page and mail it to Harlequin Reader Service®

IN U.S.A.	IN CANADA
3010 Walden Ave.	P.O. Box 609
P.O. Box 1867	Fort Erie, Ontario
Buffalo, N.Y. 14240-1867	L2A 5X3

YES! Please send me 2 free Harlequin American Romance® novels and my free surprise gift. After receiving them, if I don't wish to receive anymore, I can return the shipping statement marked cancel. If I don't cancel, I will receive 4 brand-new novels every month, before they're available in stores! In the U.S.A., bill me at the bargain price of $4.24 plus 25¢ shipping & handling per book and applicable sales tax, if any*. In Canada, bill me at the bargain price of $4.99 plus 25¢ shipping & handling per book and applicable taxes**. That's the complete price and a savings of at least 10% off the cover prices—what a great deal! I understand that accepting the 2 free books and gift places me under no obligation ever to buy any books. I can always return a shipment and cancel at any time. Even if I never buy another book from Harlequin, the 2 free books and gift are mine to keep forever.

154 HDN DZ7S
354 HDN DZ7T

Name	(PLEASE PRINT)	
Address	Apt.#	
City	State/Prov.	Zip/Postal Code

Not valid to current Harlequin American Romance® subscribers.

Want to try two free books from another series?
Call 1-800-873-8635 or visit www.morefreebooks.com.

* Terms and prices subject to change without notice. Sales tax applicable in N.Y.
** Canadian residents will be charged applicable provincial taxes and GST.
   All orders subject to approval. Offer limited to one per household.
   ® are registered trademarks owned and used by the trademark owner and or its licensee.

AMER04R   ©2004 Harlequin Enterprises Limited

eHARLEQUIN.com

The Ultimate Destination for Women's Fiction

Your favorite authors are just a click away
at www.eHarlequin.com!

- Take a sneak peek at the covers and
  read summaries of **Upcoming Books**

- Choose from over 600
  author **profiles!**

- Chat with your favorite authors
  on our **message boards.**

- Are you an author in the making?
  Get advice from published authors
  in **The Inside Scoop!**

**Learn about your favorite authors
in a fun, interactive setting—
visit www.eHarlequin.com today!**

INTAUTH04R

HARLEQUIN *Super* **ROMANCE**

They're definitely not two of a kind!

Twins

His Real Father
by **Debra Salonen**
(Harlequin Superromance #1279)

Lisa never had trouble telling the Kelly brothers
apart. Even though they were twins, they were
nothing alike. Joe was quiet and Patrick was the
life of the party. Each was important to her.
But only one was the father of her son.

Watch for it in June 2005.

Available wherever Harlequin Superromance books are sold.

www.eHarlequin.com   HSRHRF0605

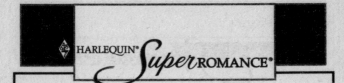

HARLEQUIN *Super*ROMANCE

Stranger in Town
by
brenda novak

(Superromance #1278)

Read the latest installment in Brenda Novak's series about the people of Dundee, Idaho: STRANGER IN TOWN.

Gabe Holbrook isn't really a stranger, but he might as well be. After the accident—caused by Hannah Russell—he's been a wheelchair-bound recluse. Now Hannah's in his life again…and she's trying to force him to live again.

Critically acclaimed novelist Brenda Novak brings you another memorable and emotionally engaging story. Come home to Dundee—or come and visit, if you haven't been there before!

Available in June 2005 wherever Harlequin books are sold.

www.eHarlequin.com

HSRNOVAK0605

HARLEQUIN®

 AMERICAN *Romance*®

Catch the latest story in the bestselling miniseries by

Tina Leonard

 *Cowboys* BY **THE DOZEN!**

When Holly Henshaw, wedding planner extraordinaire, ended up alone at the altar, she decided then and there: no more true love. Adventure, excitement, freedom—that's what she wanted. Then she met Bandera Jefferson. The cowboy was ornery, possessive…and sexy as the dickens. Now, wild-at-heart Holly has begun to think she just might like belonging to Bandera.

BELONGING TO BANDERA

Harlequin American Romance #1069

Available June 2005.

And don't miss—

CROCKETT'S SEDUCTION

Harlequin American Romance #1083

Coming in September 2005.

www.eHarlequin.com   HARBELBAN

HARLEQUIN®

AMERICAN *Romance*®

SARAH'S GUIDE TO LIFE, LOVE & GARDENING

by Connie Lane

(Harlequin American Romance #1072)

When Sarah Allcroft comes across an opportunity to be a gardener at Cupid's Hideaway, an Ohio bed-and-breakfast, she jumps at it. And when she meets the handsome local police chief, she realizes she might be able to brush up on more than her gardening.

Available in June 2005 wherever Harlequin books are sold.

www.eHarlequin.com

HARSGLLG